Birdie

&

Jude

BY

Phyllis H. Moore

http://www.phyllishmoore.com

Dedication

This story is dedicated to

Rev. Ronnie Green

and

Sam Shaw, RIP

In the late 1960's two young black men, students, successful athletes, and citizens, were taken to a cemetery by eight white men. Ropes were placed around their necks, and their families were threatened if they ever spoke of the incident. Lives and livelihoods were compromised. The two young men were friends. Their final two years of high school were filled with fear and anxiety, according to one of them. However, their faith inspired them to higher callings, and they learned this incident didn't have to define their adult lives. They moved into roles of mentoring and coaching other young men, fought for their country, preached, and put aside any ill feelings toward the eight men who threatened them in their youth. Most of those men are now deceased.

I regret the way the community treated those young men, the community where they grew up, a community that wanted to watch them on the football field but didn't want to acknowledge they were human. It was a community I was part of also, one that still thrills to the sound of the band playing *Dixie*.

Their crime, friendships with white girls, threw a panic into the men who threatened the boys. It was difficult to accept the duplicity of being honored on the athletic field and threatened as people. "Blacks stood at the gym, Mexicans at the auditorium and the whites were in the middle. It seems I was at school to perform on the field, track, and the basketball court. Nothing else mattered." This quote by Ronnie Green probably resonates with other young men, now, and then.

There was no communication except threats because that was the language used for such situations. That's no excuse for what happened to those boys. The men who made the threats knew better. They were acting from a position of power and fear. They threatened because they could, and there were no words to define their feelings. They, too, were just as vulnerable as those boys. However, they were cowards in their failure to attempt a common language. They were supposed to be role models and mentors. They were racists.

To this day whites who attended the very same school will say there was never racism in that community. Some of those eight white men have said it. It could be denial or possibly shame, but whatever it is, it's what's wrong with our society.

CHAPTER 1

BIRDIE

SHE DIDN'T KNOW it yet, but this day would be a peculiar one for Birdie Barnes. Her routine would be altered, her reserve would be challenged, and she would never think of herself in the same way. She often looked for signs to make sense of the world, and today she would find them. The question would be, would she again fail to recognize herself in her own story?

Birdie held her breath, watching as the weatherman stood in front of the state of Texas, making a circular motion with his right hand. A swirl of white hovered in the Gulf of Mexico parallel with his waist, as his head barely touched Dallas. Birdie balanced on the edge of the sofa, Ollie at her feet. Ollie's morning walk was overdue, but Birdie didn't want to miss the update on the latest tropical disturbance. The thought of another devastating storm tearing at the side of her home and water filtering in through antique windows gave her a fit of anxiety. She had just gotten her life back in order from the last onslaught of wind and rain.

"Okay, come on, Ollie. This may be our last chance for a walk on the beach. It looks like that storm is going to hang there and brew itself into something worrisome. I like my little island, but these damn storms drive me nuts. I'm getting too old for such nonsense.

"Mama and Daddy would be out buying vodka for a martini party if they were here, but they're long gone, so we have to come up with a better plan." Birdie muttered under her breath as she gathered the things she needed for the walk. She was distracted by the threat of a storm. Taking deep breaths to gather her thoughts. *What do I need to do today to get ready?* She walked into the vestibule for Ollie's leash.

Ollie didn't move until Birdie came into the room for a second time. He knew her habits. She would always return, forgetting one thing or another, cursing him under her breath the whole time she was roaming the rooms. He rolled his eyes and watched her until he saw her pick up the keys—that was the signal. They would, indeed, be leaving the house.

The keys weren't for the car. They would walk to the beach. Birdie always locked the front door. She had done that since her friend, Cami, had returned from working in her potting shed and discovered someone in her house. It turned out to be a disoriented homeless person, but still, the way Cami described the surprise was unsettling. They recognized most of the local homeless and Birdie often held conversations with them, but the man in Cami's house had been a stranger, not from close by.

Birdie had her keys in one hand, Ollie's leash and her sunhat in the other. The dog stood and stretched. Birdie leaned down to attach the leash to his collar, balancing her elbow on her knee to heave herself up. Some days were better than others. Most days, arthritis bothered her.

After locking the door, Birdie dropped the keys into the pocket of the long smock top she wore over cropped jeans. Her flip-flops weren't practical for walking, but she still enjoyed wearing them. Her nephew frequently complained that she was going to twist her ankles and needed practical shoes. He had given her a pair of black leather lace-up shoes for Christmas. She waited until he left to drop them off at the charity resale shop on Broadway. He meant well; however, she often felt irritated with him. They looked like old lady shoes. Birdie couldn't slip them off and walk to the edge of the water, feeling the sand between her toes. What was he thinking? Yes, she was an older lady, but she didn't have to wear the shoes.

Barry, Birdie's nephew, was attentive to her. His parents had been killed in an automobile accident on the causeway coming back from Houston; a drunk had rear-ended them, sending them over the railing and into the intracoastal canal. Barry was in college at the time, and as their only surviving child required Birdie's emotional support.

Birdie had never married and, with no children of her own, was happy to be there for Barry. She felt a responsibility to her brother and sister-in-law. Now he was in his early thirties and Birdie was ready for him to find another woman besides her; his monthly visits smothered her.

One Sunday each month, Barry would arrive with flowers and escort Birdie to church services. She'd never told him that she didn't enjoy church, but she went to accommodate Barry's need to be seen assisting her in her old age. She put on the same dress, her only one, and sat dutifully by him, staring at the backs of the heads of people she had grown to loathe. She had become irritated with the squabbles over preachers, petty gossiping, and the latest scandal among the parishioners. It was always some salacious event that could easily have taken place in one of the soap operas her mother had watched as a young woman. Birdie found herself sitting in the pew wondering where the people around her got their sex drive. She found them off-putting and

had seen the outline of the boy clearly, riding with no hands gripping the handlebars, guiding the bike with his balance, and swerving quickly to avoid the roots of old oaks heaving sections of the sidewalk up in large chunks. Birdie turned and looked again, pushing her sunglasses up to get a better look. There was no bicycle, but more disappointing, there was no boy.

Was the vision a distant memory, or was the boy riding so fast he was out of sight by the time she turned her head? Surely boys could still ride down her street. The live oaks towered above, casting shadows on the pavement. Some of their branches reached across the street and formed a tunnel with the trees on the opposite side. Birdie stared at them, remembering riding her own bike down the middle of the street, daring any vehicle to approach her and ruin her moment.

She looked at the windows of her house, wondering if she should get someone to check and lower her hurricane blinds. She always feared rolling down a bird's nest full of eggs or a rat carcass. She would call Don Roberts when she returned from her walk and see if he could drop by. She would rather take care of the task early and get it out of the way. Birdie made a mental note to check the supplies. She thought she might have drinking water left from the last storm. Birdie tried to compile a mental grocery list—things not requiring refrigeration or heating, maybe canned meats and some beans, cold cereal and such. Her mental notes often escaped her memory after a few minutes and any distraction.

The breeze was from the southeast, and Ollie stopped and held his nose into the wind. His fine terrier hair moved in wisps. It was Birdie's favorite thing to watch as he stood still. He gave his coat a good shake before heading off toward the beach. He nosed around an Oleander shrub. Birdie smiled to herself. He wasn't going to do his business there; he was so predictable and set in his ways. She held the leash, putting no pressure on Ollie's collar. He always stayed on the sidewalk and stopped at the crosswalk.

She could hear the surf before she could see it. There would no doubt be surfers out on the water taking advantage of the higher-than-usual waves. As they approached the seawall, there were a few surfers, and tourists still roamed the seawall and rode on surreys and bicycles.

Birdie preferred the beach after most of the tourists left. The traffic was less hectic, and there were times when she and Ollie were the only ones there. She had a tennis ball in her pocket to throw for fetch. He was only good for two or three throws, and then he would turn and look at her through his long eyebrows as if to say, "Really, Birdie, can't I just enjoy the view?"

Sometimes Birdie could actually hear his sarcasm. No one would ever accuse Ollie of being a cuddly companion, but

Birdie enjoyed him and his bad attitude. They made a good couple.

Ollie led Birdie down a sloping concrete ramp and onto the beach. They walked east and Birdie held her head up into the wind, enjoying the morning sun on her face. There was a sunbather down the beach. Birdie would encourage Ollie to turn around and head west before they reached the lone person.

There was something odd about the scene; the closer they walked, Birdie could tell the body was prone but clothed, and seemed to be injured. The position of the body wasn't the normal posture of a sunbather. There was a gauze bandage on one of their calves, and it was stained with blood.

Ollie tugged on the leash, begging to get closer. Birdie wasn't as eager. She allowed herself to be pulled closer and the figure didn't stir. It was a young woman with a slender build and long hair splayed on the sand. Birdie spoke to Ollie aloud, hoping to rouse the girl. There was no movement. Ollie walked close, sniffing and whining.

"Oh heavens, and I've left the house without the damn phone."

CHAPTER 2

JUDE

THE SUN FELT bright on the young woman's face and cast a gray-white scene on the inside of her eyelids. The sound of the surf was the white noise she'd needed—a rhythm of nothing to help her escape. A shadow moved over her face. She could feel the temperature cool and see the lightness behind her eyes darken. It might be the sun going behind a cloud, but then she felt something else; there was someone beside her and something lower, closer to her face. They were talking. Someone was talking.

Jude opened one eye and saw a furry coat of tan and white. When she opened both eyes and turned her head, she saw the ears and eyes of a dog staring directly at her. The sniffing nose approached her head, and she watched as the nostrils fluctuated with each breath. She saw a jerk of the collar and heard the dog's tags jingle as he was tugged by the woman who peered down above him. The glare of the sun only allowed Jude to see a dark figure, the outline of a large sunhat moving and swaying.

"Thank God you're alive. I forgot to bring my phone and I thought I might have to run back to the street and flag someone down. I'm not up for that, so I'm so glad you were just napping. You were just napping, right?"

"I'm okay. Well, I'm not okay, but I'm not dead," Jude said, sitting up and brushing the sand from her sleeves. She rubbed the bandage on her leg and exposed bruising on her lower arms.

"What happened to you?" Birdie asked. "You're pretty banged up."

"Yeah, I just got out of the hospital. It's been a tough two days. I think it's been two days. I didn't know where to go, so I came here to try to collect my thoughts. I guess I fell asleep. There was no sleep in that emergency room, and… well, let's just say I've lost track of time and any motivation to care about anything. So, I laid down here, and here I am, wherever this is."

"Your hair has blood caked in it, young lady. You should probably wash up and get those wounds clean. I'm not a nurse, but you might get an infection or something."

Jude winced, looking up at Birdie and squinting at the brightness behind her. "I'm sorry I startled you. I guess I should be moving on before I upset someone else. I just needed to rest.

I can sit here a few minutes and then maybe get a cab or something."

"I'm sorry, sweetie. I know I should be more helpful, but I tend to jump right to the crust of the biscuit. I'm Birdie, and this is my dog, Ollie. We're on our morning walk and live just up 15th Street. We would like to invite you for some toast and coffee or tea. I would be happy to help you with your situation if I can."

"I don't expect you can help. I'm not sure what my next step is. I have to think on it."

"Well, it's always better to think with something in your stomach. If you can manage to stand on that leg and walk, Ollie and I will be willing to walk with you and talk about it."

"Okay, if you're not going to give up, I guess I should probably talk this out with someone. I waited for the social worker to show up to interview me in the ER, but it was taking too long, and I really needed to get out of there."

Jude stood and managed to limp along with Birdie up the ramp and across the seawall to 15th Street. They made small talk, and Jude told Birdie she was aware there was a storm strengthening in the Gulf. It had been a major topic of conversation in the ER between nurses and the doctor. After they told her Casey hadn't made it, they were less talkative and left her alone in the room, telling her she would be visited by a social worker.

She had tried to stay awake, unable to process what had happened. The doctor had delivered more bad news about her own condition. The injuries were the least of her problems. He had strongly advised a visit with the social worker and asked that she remain in the room until they could arrange it. Two hours later, she'd put her clothes on and walked out, straight down 9th Street until she reached the beach.

"So where did you park your car?" Birdie asked.

"I don't know what happened to the car," Jude admitted. "I was in a fatal accident. My friend is deceased. It wasn't my car, but I was told all the vehicles were taken off by wreckers."

"Oh my." Birdie's eyes widened. "I'm so sorry, sweetie. You have had a bad time, haven't you? Well, there's nothing to do, but you come home with me, and we'll get you squared away. I'm not taking no for an answer. You're probably still in shock, for heaven's sake." Birdie looked into Jude's eyes.

Jude stared as Birdie flinched and looked away. There was something familiar about the reaction. Maybe it was the blood in her hair. She hadn't looked in a mirror since the restroom at the convenience store she and Casey stopped at on IH45. She must look a mess.

She probably was in shock. Jude felt out of herself, unable to think about what she should do, or where she should go. It didn't help that she had been in the midst of the biggest transition in her life. She and Casey were celebrating their newfound freedom, planning to embark on an adventure.

Birdie led the way, no longer talking. Jude limped behind and Birdie glanced back often to check on her. Ollie trotted toward home, not glancing back at either of them. He was on a mission. Maybe Birdie was in a hurry to get home, possibly thinking Jude wouldn't make it that far. *What must I look like to this lady?*

The houses behind the commercial buildings on the seawall were Victorian, painted in sherbet colors with filigreed gingerbread trims in white. There were copper awnings, wide porches, and tropical plants behind low front fences, a hidden part of the city Jude hadn't seen during her short stay. She had admired the stately mansions on Broadway, but these quaint, two-story cottages had been veiled in neighborhoods off the beaten path.

Ollie turned into an alley and up brick steps under a large oak tree. Birdie turned to Jude. "This is my humble abode. Come on up." She motioned to a wide porch up several steps. There were potted palms and wicker furniture situated on the porch in a pleasing conversation area. A large hanging bed filled the space on the side porch. Jude longed to slump against the plump pillows and let her eyes close again. She'd never felt so exhausted. How could her eyes possibly flutter closed while she was standing?

"That bed looks so inviting," Jude said. She barely recognized the sound of her voice, sluggish and deep. Maybe it was the shot the nurse had given her before telling her someone would come to talk with her.

"It's waiting just for you," Birdie said. "First, let's get you some nourishment and a shower."

"Oh, I don't know about the shower. I just need to figure out—"

"Nonsense, a shower will help you think. I've solved most of my problems in the shower. No offense, but you look like hell, sweetie. You haven't even told me your name."

"I'm sorry. You're right. I can't think. My name is Judith Reynolds. Most people call me Jude."

"That's a great name. I'm going to like saying 'Hey, Jude.' Come on inside. You can sit in the kitchen while I get our breakfast together."

Birdie led Jude into the black-and-white tiled foyer with a coatrack where she hung Ollie's leash. She hung her sun hat on a brass wall hook and placed her keys in a dish on the hall tree.

She led Jude through a comfortable living area to French doors on the back of the house and let Ollie out.

"He knows he'll get his breakfast when we've eaten," Birdie said. "I'm the boss around here." She grinned at Jude, then looked away quickly. Again, there was an inability to look her in the eye. There was something familiar, but Jude knew she had never seen Birdie before. The refusal to look at her might be the guilt of the foster parents who had opened their homes to her as a child and then, for some reason, asked that she be moved. It was a fleeting look, leaving Jude with a hollow feeling. A notion that there was a bit of pity behind the faces, but no commitment.

Birdie motioned Jude toward a roomy breakfast area with a large open kitchen with copper pots hanging from the ceiling. The breakfast table was round, pushed up to an L-shaped banquette upholstered in a bright floral print. There were three mismatched chairs painted red, turquois, and yellow around the outside of the table. The room was a warm mustard color, with black-and-white tile flooring. Jude thought it looked like a court jester's outfit, bright and witty. The cabinets were a dark ebony topped with white marble. She recognized canisters and other pieces by a popular pottery designer. The knobs on the drawers and doors matched the canisters.

"I love that designer." Jude pointed to Birdie's canisters.

17

"Oh, you know of her? Yes, I'm a collector. I like the whimsical feel of her pieces. I had the kitchen remodeled a couple of years ago and used her pottery pieces as inspiration. My nephew cautioned me about being too bold, but I can say after a couple of years, I'm not tired of it. It still makes me smile to walk in here."

The visual stimulation of the kitchen bolstered Jude, as Birdie busied herself preparing coffee, scrambling eggs, and making toast. Jude slid into a spot on the banquette. Butter and jelly were placed in front of her. Birdie sat across from Jude after placing a plate of eggs and toast at each of their places.

"Now eat up, Jude. You're going to need your strength for this day. It may not be an easy day, but you'll face it with nourishment, or my name's not Bernadette Roberta Barnes."

"Bernadette Roberta? I thought you told me your name was Birdie?" Jude picked up a piece of toast and began spreading it with a dollop of soft butter. She dipped a spoon into the jelly and plopped it next to the toast on her plate. Her arms felt like lead, heavy and cumbersome.

"Birdie's a nickname. Can you imagine naming a baby Bernadette Roberta? Luckily my father thought I looked like a baby bird and started calling me Birdie."

Jude asked questions about Birdie's house and neighborhood while they ate. She chewed slowly, aware her lips were swollen and the inside of her mouth raw. Birdie answered, giving the history of the family home, telling Jude she had been raised in the house.

"Barry's my only living relative. He's my brother's boy. So I suppose when I'm gone, this will be Barry's house. He'll be free to repaint the kitchen if he doesn't like it."

It was a comfortable house. Jude continued chewing cautiously, wincing at the pain in her mouth. She had forgotten the last time she had eaten anything, but it must have been before the incident outside the convenience store.

Jude glanced into the large room next to the kitchen, admiring it. The living area they walked through had been lined with bookcases and decorated with overstuffed furniture, not the fragile-looking Victorian pieces Jude had seen in other such houses. The furniture was slipcovered in white with large plump needlepoint pillows. The wide-planked wooden floors were covered in soft oriental rugs in red and gold hues. The tall windows were covered with louvered shutters, the slats tilted to allow filtered light into the room. The back windows had open shutters and faced a large screened porch furnished with wrought iron and wicker furniture. Newspapers and magazines were piled on an ottoman on the porch. She could picture Birdie sitting there overlooking the back courtyard, relaxing with Ollie.

"You have a nice quiet life in this cozy house, don't you, Birdie?" Jude said, continuing to glance out the back windows. She had offered to help Birdie clean up after their breakfast, but Birdie insisted she take it easy.

"I'm very comfortable, and I like my life. However… well, let's just say I'm glad Ollie and I came across you on the beach this morning. It's a little like stumbling upon a mermaid." Birdie looked Jude in the eye this time and didn't look away. It was Jude's turn to flinch. She had seen Birdie's eyes before, but she didn't know where. She could swear those eyes had looked into hers and there was recognition.

It wasn't common for Jude to know someone's gaze. Almost everyone she had lived with since childhood was a stranger, never seeing her long enough to recognize she could be a part of their family. It was a silent rejection she had become accustomed to. Birdie must have known the quick avoidance. Now, she was looking back.

Jude laughed. She hardly considered herself a mermaid. She felt more like an injured dolphin or something, disoriented, out of her habitat, confused. "I'm no mermaid. I think if I had one of those lovely tails, it might be torn."

"Nothing some antiseptic and a shower can't fix. If that doesn't work, I believe I can locate some duct tape."

Birdie filled a metal bowl with water and pointed to the back porch. Jude watched her empty a packet of food into a bowl for Ollie. She stepped onto the porch and looked out to the courtyard. There were various tropical plants in concrete containers. A small koi pond and a seating area were surrounded by a brick patio.

"Who takes care of all of the plants, Birdie?"

"I enjoy doing that." Birdie smiled. "That's how I spend my day, watering, dead-heading, thinning, and repotting. I like to dig in the dirt. I always have. My mother was a gardener. She spent almost all day outside, working and sitting to admire her work. Her favorite thing to do was entertain out here. Of course, that was a different time. She had help inside, cleaning and cooking. Those were the days when we ate our main meal at noon when my father would come home for lunch. He walked to work to the pharmacy on Broadway. He would come home for lunch, take a short nap, and then walk back to work until about six. There was no air conditioning. The windows were wide open, and we enjoyed that lovely gulf breeze."

Jude watched Birdie's face as she talked. She was lost in the memory of childhood summers. It was pleasant to listen to Birdie reminisce. It took Jude's mind off her own problems for a while. However, when Birdie's voice stopped, reality returned. Jude needed to think about what she was going to do.

"What are you looking at?" Jude asked.

"I'm thinking I'm tired of looking at that clump of dried blood in your hair. I wish you'd take a shower."

"I guess I should. People will probably be afraid of me if I wander around looking like this. I don't want to inconvenience you, but I would appreciate using your shower and some shampoo."

"It's no inconvenience. I'll show you to the upstairs bathroom. I keep it ready for guests. I don't have many—guests, that is—but I like to keep it prepared."

Birdie led Jude to the second floor up the main staircase. She said there was another landing at the back of the hall that would take her to a narrower stairway into the butler's pantry on the first floor. Birdie showed Jude to a bedroom overlooking a second-floor balcony facing 15th Street. The room was filled with light, furnished with an iron bed and a mix of old oak furniture. Painted a pale, dusty blue, the bedroom had long white shutters on the windows.

Birdie opened a wardrobe and pulled out a white terrycloth robe. She held it up in front of her. "This is probably too big for your petite frame, but it's something to wear while I get your clothes washed up."

"Oh, you don't need to bother with that, Birdie. I'll be fine until I can get some clothes."

"No sense in washing your body and then putting on dirty clothes. You were asleep on the beach, for heaven's sake. Now, don't argue with me." Birdie gave Jude a serious, parental stare. "Put this robe on after your shower and bring me those dirty clothes for the wash. If I act fast, I think I can get the blood out of those jeans. I'll show you where the antiseptic is and you can doctor those cuts. You'll find soap and shampoo and a stack of towels on the shelves in the bathroom. After you have a shower, I think you should take a nap and get some rest. Don't make any major decisions without some rest."

Jude nodded, unable to respond. The thought of being able to get some sleep was enticing. It made her yawn just thinking about it. She couldn't remember the last time she'd slept in a real bed. If she attempted to respond to Birdie's instructions, she might start weeping. Although it was hard to believe she hadn't yet found the energy to cry. Where were her tears? They flooded her mind but wouldn't spill over into her eyes. Where was the emotion allowing them to pour? She feared, once they began, she couldn't stop.

Jude was motionless as Birdie left the room. The day had not been what she'd anticipated. It wasn't just the day, it was everything that happened since she graduated and left on the trip with Casey. Nothing was going as planned. She didn't have time to think about Casey's death, too busy thinking about herself.

What will I do? Losing Casey was a blow, but the other news took her breath away. She would sleep and then try to pull something from her addled brain. Could she make sense of what happened? A cleansing cry might help, but she couldn't summon the strength.

CHAPTER 3

BIRDIE

THE WASHER AGITATED Jude's clothing. Birdie could hear its sloshing sounds in the laundry room next to the kitchen. She placed a batch of cookies in the oven and set the timer before sitting at the breakfast table with the crossword puzzle. She planned to be there to hear her yellow duck timer go off with a quack when the cookies were done. Barry had given her the timer as a gag gift. She grinned. Birdie appreciated the duck much more than the costly leather shoes he'd purchased for her. *Silly boy, he could have saved ninety dollars.*

Birdie's morning activity had been much busier than her normal schedule. With the approach of the storm and finding Jude on the beach, she still had much to accomplish before noon. She didn't mind the break in the monotony. It was different, but it was also a spark, something she had needed for a while—a reason to vary the mundane.

Birdie looked up from the puzzle, staring at the plastic yellow duck on the kitchen counter, the faint ticking a reminder of the seconds clicking past. *If I hadn't found Jude, the storm would have forced me into action, or maybe the cruise. Something would have.* She wanted to believe she wasn't so predictable as the next click of the timer.

Across the room, the television was muted. She could follow the tropical storm announcements scrolling across the screen. She watched the screen, the weather map prominent. Birdie crossed the room to increase the volume. The storm had been upgraded to a category one. There were spaghetti models indicating landfall anywhere between Brownsville and New Orleans.

"Great," Birdie said under her breath. "High anxiety for anyone in that broad area. Okay, Ollie, we go into our A plan for this afternoon." Birdie decided to walk to the corner market after the current batch of cookies were done. She would get the supplies she had thought about earlier and plan on Jude sheltering with her. The girl had no transportation, and it would be difficult to arrange with the storm approaching.

She wrote a note to leave on the kitchen table in case Jude came down while she was gone. Birdie turned the oven off, even though there was more cookie dough for future batches in the refrigerator. She put her wallet and phone in the pocket of her smock, trusting she could recall her mental list once she entered the market. Glancing at Ollie, she gave him the signal for stay. He rolled his eyes. She had no leash, and he wouldn't be making the trip with her.

Birdie took the alley to the back of the market, wanting to avoid Velma Ritter. Velma always watched from her porch in the afternoon and would try to entice Birdie over to catch up on the latest gossip. For the past year, that gossip was a litany of the acquaintances deceased since their last visit and Velma's opinion of the "tacky" plans for their funeral. She had no intention of engaging Velma. There was too much to do.

She entered the store focused, hoping she didn't meet anyone expecting a conversation. She would have trouble explaining her plans for the storm without arousing worry and comments. After all, she had taken in a stranger. Her neighbors wouldn't understand her assurances that Jude was perfectly harmless.

She avoided the cereal aisle, where Joe DeMac was restocking the shelves. She would get other items first and then recheck that aisle. She put three bottles of wine in her basket; she didn't know if Jude drank, but she intended to. Birdie recalled a lasagna casserole in the freezer. She would heat it for dinner with a green salad and some bread. It was always nice with a good merlot.

Comfort food was on Birdie's mind. She gravitated to the chips and candy aisles, where she placed several bags of each in the handbasket. By the time she visited the canned meats, Joe had left the cereal. Milk, bread, candles, and batteries and Birdie headed for one of two check-out stands.

"Hey, Birdie. Barry must be coming to spend the storm with you," Mr. Randle said.

"No, I haven't heard what Barry's plans are, but I'm stocking up. It's the season, and I don't want to have to keep coming back to the store. Might as well be ready for anything."

Mr. Randle nodded. Birdie was one of a handful of neighbors continuing to shop in his store. Most of the neighborhood drove farther down the seawall to a modern chain grocery taking advantage of fresh-made sushi, a refrigerated counter full of prepared meals, and lower prices.

"Thank you kindly for your business, Birdie. You stay safe now. Where's Ollie? I haven't seen you without your little companion. You know we always have a biscuit for him."

"He's napping. I didn't want to disturb him."

"Take him a biscuit anyway," Mr. Randle insisted, handing Birdie a dog biscuit. She dropped it into her pocket. "You stay safe now, and let us know if you need anything. Let me get Rita to bring these things by later. It's too much for you to carry. I'd help you, but I'm the only one here right now. I just sent Joe down to Sims."

"Oh, I'll be fine with most of this, but you can bring the wine by. You stay safe, too, George. Don't stay open thinking you have to. Take care of yourself and Rita. Everyone's been warned. It's up to them to be prepared."

Birdie exited the store, the groceries were taxing her shopping bags. It was a good decision to consent to delivery for the wine. She walked quickly, hoping the bags didn't break. She usually only picked up a few items. She thought George was right, Barry hadn't made contact with her since the latest reports on the storm. It wasn't like him. He might be traveling, as he often did for his job, and hadn't been watching the local news.

Several steps down the alley, Birdie felt her phone vibrating in her pocket. She couldn't stop to answer; the shopping bags were awkward. *I'll just have to check my voice mail when I get home.*

"Oh shit."

Velma was walking past the alley exit with her poodle. She glanced down the lane, waved to Birdie, and waited.

"Hey, Velma," Birdie said, picking up her pace. "I'm sorry I can't dally. I have ice cream in my bag and need to get home to put it in the freezer."

"Well, Birdie, that's not going to do you any good if the electricity goes off. You're going to have to eat that stuff tonight. It's just going to melt."

"Think positive, Velma. Sorry, I really have to run. You stay safe. We'll chat after the storm situation resolves."

She knew she was waddling as she hurried away with the bags. Birdie didn't look back. She thought any eye contact would lock Velma in, and she would never get away from her. Birdie continued to walk at a faster pace until she reached the steps. Carefully balancing the heavy bags as she mounted the treads to the porch, she loosened one bag and let it fall to the floor. She left it on the porch as she entered her front door, finding Ollie napping on his pillow.

The house smelled of fresh baked chocolate chip cookies. Birdie placed the shopping bag on the breakfast table and returned to the porch for the other bag. The postman was climbing her steps and handed her the mail. "Afternoon, Ms. Barnes. You getting ready for this storm?"

"Yes, Benny, I've just been to the store to stock up."

Benny glanced at the bag. "You really know how to weather a storm."

Birdie glanced down and smiled, tilting her head.

"All right, I understand." Benny said.

"Stay safe, Benny. Watch the weather and plan accordingly. You remember last time, you got caught on the mainland and couldn't get home."

"I will. You don't have to remind me about that. My wife never lets me live that down." Birdie knew the talk about Benny and his mainland girlfriend. *Not my business.*

Birdie entered the house with the mail and the second bag of groceries. She went to the kitchen to begin the task of putting her supplies away. Ollie stood and shook, walking to stand beside her. "Oh, you're pretty smart, aren't you? Yes, George gave me a biscuit for you. Come on out here and I'll give it to you while you're on your way out to do your business."

Birdie opened the French doors to the screened porch reaching in her pocket to give Ollie the biscuit. She examined the hinges on the shutters around the porch. Would they hold in high winds? Barry had cautioned her about needing to replace the shutters, but maybe they could weather one more storm. Birdie would have the wooden shutters around the porch latched when Don came to lower the hurricane blinds.

When she returned to the kitchen, she pulled her phone from her pocket and glanced at the phone numbers posted on her kitchen bulletin board. Running her finger down the list, she found Don Robert's number and prepared to dial. She noticed a voice mail from Barry. *That'll just have to wait until I have this business taken care of.*

By the time Birdie glanced at her watch, it was after three o'clock. She took the lasagna out of the freezer and placed it in the refrigerator. Jude had slept through lunch, and Birdie thought they might eat an early dinner.

She had a disturbing thought that Jude might have slipped out of the house while she was at the store. She tiptoed up the back stairs to peek into the guest room. Jude was on the bed under a throw, sound asleep. She had her long hair wrapped in a towel. Birdie turned and went back downstairs to continue her preparations.

A weather bulletin was scrolling across the screen when Birdie returned to the living area. Ollie was standing at the French doors peering inside. She opened the door, allowing him in, and went to turn up the volume on the television. The storm had again been upgraded. "Damn, it's one of those kinds of storms. It's going to sit in the Gulf and drive everyone crazy guessing where it will go while it just gets stronger and angrier."

An update was given on the path of the storm, and Birdie was concerned to see the eye was projected to pass right over the island. Landfall was predicted for daybreak the following day.

The seldom-used dining room had a large buffet where Birdie stored candles and oil lamps. She placed the lamps and candles on the dining room table with extra batteries and flashlights, testing the battery-operated radio.

The phone rang in Birdie's pocket. She noticed it was Velma. Birdie decided to answer, hoping she wouldn't be bothered later in the day.

"Birdie, is Barry there with you? Why don't you come over here tonight? That storm's going to be here in the morning, but you know as well as I do that means we'll start feeling the winds and rain sometime later this evening. No sense being in that big house all by yourself."

"I'm fine, Velma. I have Ollie here, and I know how you feel about other dogs around Fifi. Is Wendell there with you?"

"Yes, he is. Ollie is welcome to stay on our back porch. That's not a problem."

"Thank you for checking, Velma, but I'm really fine. I have all my supplies out. Don's coming in a while to get the hurricane blinds down. We'll be just fine. I'm just getting all the supplies together now. I'm prepared, and I'll be just fine."

"If you change your mind, don't hesitate to come over."

"Thank you, Velma. I appreciate it."

Birdie hung up quickly, not wanting to chat longer than she had to. She was just about to call Barry when someone rang the front door bell. Birdie peered out the dining room window and saw Don Roberts's truck. They exchanged greetings at the door, and Don went about securing Birdie's blinds and shutters. Birdie baked the rest of the cookie dough and cleaned up the kitchen while Don secured the windows. When he was finished, he peeked in the kitchen.

"You stay safe, Ms. Birdie. This may be a false alarm, but I think you're wise to get the blinds down and get ready." Birdie followed him to the front door, handed him a baggie of cookies, and latched the door behind him.

Birdie didn't like how dark the blinds made the interior of the house when they were secured. However, she knew they gave her a sense of safety when the winds and rains started. She turned on lamps on her way to the kitchen. By the time the cookies and shutters were complete, it was close to five.

Jude is sleeping the day away. She opened the refrigerator and took out lettuce and vegetables to make a salad. When it was complete, she covered the bowl with plastic wrap and returned it to the refrigerator. She set the table and opened a bottle of wine to let it breathe on the counter, deciding to sip on a glass while she watched the latest news on the storm.

Birdie finally settled down in her favorite chair and thought about the odd girl she had found on the beach. It was peculiar that there was something familiar about her. It was her eyes—

like looking into the soul of an old friend. She had never experienced that feeling before. Birdie considered herself an introvert, not wanting to strike up new relationships. She had many old ones, thanks to the legacy of her family. They had lived in the same place forever, so her parents' friends were her friends, as well as their children. She didn't put any effort into those relationships, none. They continued just as her daily routine did, on autopilot, no thinking required.

Birdie considered herself lucky that those friends still sought her out. If they had to depend on her initiating contact, she would never see or talk to them again. She couldn't see the point in it. If she had her way, her social life would have been much different than the one prescribed by her parents. Now here she sat, an older woman, stuck with those inherited friends, not of her choosing.

Jude, however, was different. There was a newness about her, but there was also something familiar. It was something Birdie hadn't experienced since childhood, an automatic attraction. There was a bittersweet feeling about it, something pleasant and troubling at the same time—a spark of recognition; but Birdie was confused about what she was recognizing. The conversation had been easy also. No thought required. It was like picking up with someone from the past.

She reflected on her day, a flurry of preparations. It was unlike the sameness of so many others. Yes, she had prepared for hurricanes several times, but there was an awakening. She had found Jude.

CHAPTER 4

JUDE

THE ROOM WAS darker when Jude opened her eyes. At first she thought it might be dark outside, but then she realized there was sunlight coming through small oval holes in front of the windows. There was some type of covering over them.

She sat up in the bed, her hands going to the top of her head. She was confused, then remembered a shower, removing the damp towel from her hair. Jude ran her fingers through her hair and fluffed it, noticing the long gash left on her head. She sat on the edge of the bed before attempting to stand. Her head was pounding. She remembered the nurse saying she may have aches and pains from the seat belt. There was a recommendation for aspirin and a prescription the hospital pharmacy had filled. She'd forgotten. *I should probably take something.*

Jude dug in her purse and found the bottle. She read the label. No, it couldn't be true. She needed to take the pills three times a day. How would she remember to do that? She was struck by the inconvenience of it. It made her angry. Jude closed her eyes, wishing she could open them and everything would change. All the things that happened the last three days would disappear. She would be in another life, a life without pills, and Casey would be there, laughing.

It had taken her a few minutes to remember where she had fallen asleep. She took the towel into the bathroom to look for any other items she might want to take downstairs for Birdie's laundry. Her clothes washed and folded, sat on a chair in the hall by the bedroom door. Her hostess was very accommodating.

Jude returned to the bathroom, where she dressed in her own fashionably tattered jeans and black pullover. Her white tennis shoes had been wiped clean of sand. She hung the robe on a hook in the bathroom, then held her purse in front of her, searching through it for a brush. She attempted to apply lipstick, but her lips were swollen and sore. As she stared at her face in the mirror, she remembered how they'd beeb injured. She looked away and held her hand to her throat, fighting back tears. The tears she'd longed for earlier were not the same as the ones for this pain.

Jude swallowed the lump in her throat, chastising herself for not having a plan. She wouldn't be able to follow through with traveling or any of the things she and Casey wanted to do. Casey was gone.

Jude left the bathroom and grabbed the stair rail. She could smell something cooking, something delicious. Her stomach growled.

When she reached the bottom of the stairs, she could see Birdie on the sofa watching television, sipping a glass of wine. Ollie was curled up on the floor at Birdie's feet.

Birdie looked up and smiled. "There's our sleeping beauty."

Jude had to smile back. Birdie was an endearing lady. In the short time Jude had known her, she knew she was warm, honest, and a caretaker.

Birdie stood and took the towel from Jude. "How about a glass of wine before dinner, Jude? We're having lasagna. If you're a vegetarian, you'll have to pick through the meat. I selected a nice merlot to go with it. Your hair looks beautiful, by the way."

"Birdie, you're too nice. I can't intrude on you any longer. I really must get myself out of here before the storm."

"It's too late. It's almost dark and the wind has picked up. There are rain bands just off the coast headed our way. We're shuttered up in here tight as Dick's hat band, and I don't intend to open the gates for you to get on a road to nowhere. Don't argue with me, missy. You need to recuperate, and I need company for the storm, so just settle yourself in. If you don't drink wine, that's fine by me. How about some tea or a cold glass of water?"

Jude sighed. It was hard to argue with Birdie's reasoning. Maybe talking with her over a glass of wine might give Jude some clarity about what her next steps should be. There really was no other person for her to confide in.

"Okay, if you insist," Jude relented. "I think I would enjoy a glass of wine."

Birdie smiled and took the towel to the laundry room, then returned to pour Jude a glass of wine. She had let the wine breathe in a cut crystal decanter and served it in matching glasses. Jude thought the glasses were elegant and commented on them.

"These were my mother's. I think they might've been wedding gifts. I suppose they're antiques now. I have so few occasions to use them. We'll have a toast to Gino. That's the storm's name, by the way, category two. Here's hoping he's as impotent as Velma's husband." Birdie chuckled, lifting her glass into the air. Jude clinked it with her own, laughing aloud at the toast.

"Who's Velma?"

"She's a neighbor from down the street. If you weren't here, I'd probably have to be holed up with her, her prissy poodle, and that impotent husband, Wendell. I'll probably go to Hell for being so mean. After the hurricane passes, I'll try to be nicer."

The aroma of the lasagna was even better than before. "The meal smells delicious, Birdie. Is there anything I can do to help you get ready?"

"I have everything together. The bread's ready to pop in the oven, and the salad is done. Let's just sit and have our wine for a few minutes. I know you must be starving. You slept right through lunch."

They watched the weather reports and sipped wine. Jude was hungry and thankful she was found on the beach by Birdie. She didn't know what would have become of her if Birdie hadn't noticed her. She probably would have taken a cab back to Houston, but she had no idea what to do after that. It had been a whirlwind since the accident, and she hadn't had an opportunity to process everything. She wondered if she was in shock. There was something off about the way she was processing information. She couldn't understand why she was being so compliant with Birdie. It was the only thing she could think to do.

I wonder where my backpack is.

Birdie was mesmerized by the weather reports. Jude watched her take in the news of the storm. There were predictions of unprecedented rain amounts.

Birdie shook her head and sighed. "There's nothing for us to worry over. Flooding would be my main concern, but there was a storm in 2008 that flooded most of the island and this block of houses did just fine. We're higher than most and right here behind the seawall. I'll go out on a limb and predict we're in the catbird seat."

Jude smiled. Birdie used sayings she hadn't heard before, but somehow she knew what they meant. Birdie was genuinely sweet, but she wondered why she would say such a thing about her friend Velma's husband being impotent. It didn't fit her nature as far as Jude knew. It was a little out of character. Maybe she would ask Birdie about it later, after they'd had another glass of wine.

"Okay, I'm turning this off. Gino will be here early in the morning, and he's wet and wild and that's all I need to know. Funny, I've known a Gino, lovely boy. I wouldn't name a hurricane after him." Birdie switched the channel to classical music and stood up. "You just sit there and relax, and I'm going to put the bread in the oven and toss the salad. We'll have a little dinner party in a few minutes."

"I appreciate everything you've done for me, Birdie. You've gone above and beyond what you needed to do, and I'm feeling quite comfortable here even though there's a storm approaching. Thanks for washing my clothes." Jude's eyes became misty as she talked. She hoped this wouldn't be the time her tears began to flow.

"Nonsense, child. I'm happy to do it. You gave an old woman purpose today, and that's a lot to give. Do you believe in fate?"

Jude nodded, afraid to say anything for fear her voice would crack.

"Well, I do too, and for some reason, I believe you and I were destined to meet on the beach this morning. We have seen each other before, not in this life or these bodies, but I'm convinced we've known each other in another time. I found you for a reason. There's a lesson in all this, and I'm pretty sure it's for me." Birdie smiled, patted Jude's hand, and headed to the kitchen.

Jude put her head back against the back of the chair and listened to the music. She hadn't ever been a fan of classical music, but it was pleasant to sit in a dim room and sip wine while listening to a soft piano. The house felt cozy and secure.

It was raining outside, but it was muted and didn't seem threatening.

Ollie stood and shook, looking at her, approached her and, curled up at her feet. Jude rubbed his side with her toe. She could hear Birdie humming, clinking ice into glasses, and opening the oven door. The odor of garlic wafted into the room. She felt far removed from the chaos of the past days, but it was still niggling at her—something she needed to resolve.

Birdie seemed to be a level head. Maybe she could give Jude some perspective, an objective opinion about what she should do. She wasn't completely honest about leaving the hospital. She needed to let Birdie know that they might be looking for her, but what if they wanted to know where she was? If the hospital staff could find her, anyone could find her. It wasn't really fair to Birdie, either. Could they both be in danger? She had no idea.

Jude's money and the rest of her belongings were in her backpack, and she had no idea where it was. The car had been towed, but she didn't know where. She would need to follow up on that if she expected to get her things back. How could she have forgotten about that? Her passport, driver's license, laptop, and all the money they needed for travel were in her backpack.

Jude took a big swig of wine and closed her eyes. A single tear finally rolled down her cheek.

CHAPTER 5

BIRDIE

THE WARMTH OF the buzz from the wine and the coziness of her home created a mellow, comfortable feeling in Birdie. She was glad Jude didn't put up an argument about staying for the storm. Birdie was relieved to have the company and enjoyed a little entertaining. She hadn't had occasion to pull out the good dishes and wineglasses in a while. There were no worries about the storm; Birdie was confident they would be fine.

As Birdie thought about her comforts, she transferred grated cheese to a glass compote with a serving spoon and placed it on a small dish. As she prepared to serve, she focused on presentation as well as flavor. Birdie felt good about taking the time to attend to details. She placed water goblets on the table, along with the wine decanter. Birdie admired the table setting as the rustic chandelier cast a glow, making the crystal sparkle.

"Okay, Jude. Dinner is served."

Jude came to the table, standing beside the chair a moment. A smile of appreciation curved her swollen lips. She set her wineglass down before taking a seat and unfolding the cloth napkin, placing it on her lap.

Jude had elegant movements for such a casual girl. She wore jeans and a pullover, the only clothing she had, but Birdie thought even movie stars dressed casually and understated. There was something about Jude. She had a natural beauty, not breathtaking but wholesome and fresh. Mysterious, Birdie felt, but she wasn't going to say it aloud. She was definitely not a street person, or even a regular person. There was more than mystery drawing Birdie to Jude. It was something in her spirit.

Birdie had known plenty of the city's homeless. She crossed paths daily with the same people due to her proximity to the seawall and frequent walks to the beach. She often spoke to them, and they liked seeing Ollie. She knew they had few opportunities to bathe or wash their hair. Jude had been well-groomed, except for the injuries and blood in her hair, and according to her, she had walked out of the hospital. She still wore the laminated bracelet, and there was tape residue on the back of her hand, which Birdie assumed was from the intravenous needle. She had no reason to doubt what Jude had told her. She had taken note of the details on Jude's body and compared them to her story—everything matched.

Birdie placed the lasagna slices on the plates and served the salad from the table. When they were ready to eat, she took a sip of wine. "So, tell me more about yourself, Jude. We haven't had a chance to visit."

"I'm twenty-six. I recently finished graduate school at the University of Texas. My best friend, Casey, and I were planning to take a year off and tour Europe. We had a lot in common. Neither of us have family. We struggled to get ourselves through school, working odd jobs and saving along the way. It wasn't too difficult to put our schooling first since we were older than most of the other students. We were focused on our goals."

Jude took a bite of the lasagna as Birdie watched her. Birdie thought she liked it. She wanted to ask, but she didn't want to interrupt the story.

"We met in undergraduate school and made a pact that we'd apply ourselves, and when we graduated we would reward ourselves with this trip. Setting goals with Casey helped me get through school."

"Is that the person who died in the accident?"

"Yes, they're running tests on her body. I don't know what will happen…." Jude began to get tears in her eyes.

"Stop, sweetie. I don't need to hear about this now. You go ahead and eat, and I'll tell you about me."

"Okay, maybe you're right." Jude dabbed at the corners of her eyes with her napkin. She sniffed and took another bite of lasagna.

"So, I was born and raised here in Galveston. Locals would call me a BOI, born on the island. My parents were BOIs also. That doesn't mean much to outsiders, but people around here seem to think it's special. My brother and I grew up in this very house. I know this neighborhood like the back of my hand. Most of the time, I like the predictability of my life and knowing everyone around me, but sometimes I long for an adventure and meeting new people."

Birdie tasted the lasagna and took a sip of wine. The meal was delicious, and she savored the flavors. She admired the table as she swirled the wine in her glass. Birdie was in the moment, enjoying every aspect of their shared meal. It was a feeling she strived to reproduce in every setting, but it was effortless with Jude.

"Ollie and I take a couple of walks to the beach each day. Every day I notice new things. This morning I found you, and this afternoon the tide was so far out I had to look twice to remind myself where I was. I had never seen that much water sucked back into the Gulf. I took a picture of it with my phone. I'll show you after dinner."

Birdie recalled the startling sight. It was something out of a science fiction story. She had pulled Ollie back across the seawall, cutting their walk short. Don Roberts had mentioned the scene to her, but she hadn't believed him. After he left and her chores were complete, she took a quick walk to see it for herself. She secretly wondered if it was an omen.

Jude looked up at Birdie. "This meal is delicious, Birdie. You're a good cook."

"I'm glad you like it. Thank you. I've always liked to cook, and there was a time when I was quite the entertainer." Birdie picked up the wine decanter and poured more into each of their glasses.

"So, you've mentioned a nephew," Jude said, picking up her glass and taking a sip. Birdie noticed her swirling the goblet and watching the legs of the wine. "Did you have a husband or children?"

"No, neither one. I got side-tracked. Well, it wasn't side-tracked really, more like socked in the gut. It took me some time to recover, and when I did, I wasn't the same person. I didn't think I was fit for a relationship, and I've done everything I can think of to ward off any suitor.

"I hated the Vietnam War. I still do. It doesn't have a thing to do with disrespecting those who served and gave their life. My life was changed, and so were thousands of others', and for what? What do we fight for? Where is the honor in killing? When I was young and foolish, I would join the marches and protests and shout my discontent. In hindsight, I'd do that all again. War is a ridiculous folly. Mankind will get that one of these days, but I know I won't live to see it. I hope you do."

"I hope I do, too." Jude pushed her plate back and folded her napkin, placing it on the table. She sat back against the banquette, holding her wineglass in both hands. "When people talk about their lives, they do seem to talk about their losses. I guess that's what makes us who we are."

Birdie nodded. "Yes, but I have so many things to be grateful for. I live on an island, for heaven's sake. Never mind that we're battened down for a hurricane. Most of the time it's quite pleasant, and I love my life here in this old house with Ollie."

Birdie's phone rang. She was slow to get up to answer. She thought about ignoring it, but since there was a storm, she didn't want to miss something important. It was Barry's number, but when she said hello, there was no response. She redialed and got no connection. "Huh, I wonder if the storm is playing havoc with the phone reception. Do you have a phone, Jude?"

"I do, but I turned it off a couple of days ago. I'd like to talk with you about that. I've been trying to think what to do. It's really helped to be able to be here and feel safe—"

Birdie's phone rang again, and that time Barry was talking before she had a chance to say anything. He was speaking quickly and asking Birdie if she was okay. "Yes, yes, Barry, I'm fine. I've got the storm blinds down and I'm quite comfortable. I have a friend here with me, so don't worry."

Jude watched while Birdie continued to talk with Barry. After a short while, she stood and began clearing the table, taking dishes to the sink. Birdie listened, not speaking to Barry's concerns, then tried to assure him that she would be fine. She later told Jude that he was in Chicago on business and had just heard of the storm's strength and landfall.

"He feels bad that he wasn't paying attention. I missed a call from him earlier, I should've realized he would be fretting about the weather and called him back. Sometimes I think he's a pest, but I'm so lucky to have him worrying after me. Poor guy's just trying to do the right thing. He doesn't get that this telephone isn't as important to me as it is to you young people. He's glancing at his constantly and would never miss a call. I don't know where the damn thing is half the time."

"He sounds sweet," Jude said. She stood by the sink with a dishcloth thrown over her shoulder. Birdie smiled at the sight of her.

"I suppose he is. He's handsome as all get-out, too. Looks just like my brother at that age. I'll show you pictures later. I'll put the food away and we can leave the dishes in the sink."

"No way. I'll wash. This cheese will be hard as a rock. I can do this part while you're putting things where they go."

"You're right. We can get this done and go sit in the den with some cookies. I want to hear more about what you started to say before."

Birdie thought Jude owed her some explanation. She had taken her into her home. The girl didn't seem to have another plan. Birdie was a spur-of-the-moment type, but Jude's situation seemed to be more than that, maybe a significant tragedy. She could be in shock. The comment about her cell phone made Birdie's ears perk up, but she didn't want to jump on that with too much enthusiasm; she knew from some of her volunteer work that it was the quickest way to encourage someone to shut down.

CHAPTER 6

JUDE

JUDE POURED HERSELF another glass of wine and relaxed into one of the two overstuffed chairs in the den. She tilted her head back and took a deep breath. Closing her eyes, she enjoyed the calm around her, aware the wind was now ripping and bending the palm trees outside. Birdie had stepped out onto the porch to retrieve a large pot that had blown over and was rolling around, pounding against the porch railing.

When Birdie entered the room, she was fluffing her damp hair, wiping the curling tendrils from her forehead. "That wind is relentless. The limbs of that big oak out front are whipping around in a frenzy. I hope I don't lose any of those bigger branches. I enjoy the shade on the yard. It's a chore getting them picked up if they snap off. Hopefully this is the worst of it."

Birdie picked up the remote and changed the channel to the local news station, where a weather map gave the latest coordinates for the storm. "Sure enough. Look at that. Those bands are circling right over us. It's not the worst of it. That won't be for a few hours, but we'll be fine."

Jude was counting on Birdie's optimism being true. She had never been through a hurricane. Her experiences had been in the Texas panhandle with tornadoes. Those storms blew over quickly. She and one of her foster families would crawl into a storm shelter and wait. This storm promised to last all night and into the next day.

Birdie muted the television. "So, where were we? You were saying you turned your phone off, and you wanted to talk about that."

"Yes, I'm worried that someone could track me if it's on. I'm not really up on how all that technology works, but I've seen such things on television." Jude took a sip of wine.

"Here, have a cookie," Birdie offered. "Sometimes sugar helps."

Jude smiled. "I wish I could go back in time and change things, but I keep replaying it in my mind, and I don't know what I'd do if I had it all to do again."

"Start from the beginning, Jude. Tell me about how you and your friend got to Galveston and what you were doing."

Casey had been excited when she came home from her shift at the café. Jude had showered and had been sitting on the sofa painting her nails, a towel wrapped around her damp hair. It had been a hot muggy day; the window unit had struggled to keep their small apartment cool. There had been good tips, and Casey smiled as she waved the bills in front of Jude. "We're this much closer to our adventure."

"We have to graduate first, Miss Priss." Jude cocked her head at Casey. "I'm still a little worried about taking off with no job to return to."

"It'll be fine. Have some faith. We'll have our degrees and the experience of foreign travel. Anyone in their right mind will want to hire us. Don't give it another thought."

Jude did admire Casey's outlook and spirit for adventure. She had always thought things would work out for the best.

The phone had rung and Jude started to answer it, but Casey waved her off, shaking her head. "It's Jax. I don't want to talk to him. I left the café early because I knew he would come in at the end of my shift. Sure enough, I saw his bike down the street when I was leaving, and I ducked out of sight. He was looking for me. This isn't going to be an easy breakup."

"I thought you both agreed."

"Let's just say I'm more agreeable than he is." Casey walked to the window, tilting the blinds to peek out. "He just needs some time to get used to it."

"You're not afraid of him, are you, Casey? I mean, he has all those biker friends. They can be a pretty rough crowd."

"I'll be fine. Let's take one day at a time and focus on our plans. Nothing can change those."

Casey had remained positive, but Jude was worried. She'd never liked Jax. He was too wild and unpredictable. Casey had thought he was exciting. She always had like the bad boys. He had been too old for Casey, in Jude's opinion. She'd wanted him to calm down and have steady employment. However, in Austin, there was a diverse group of people on the music scene and in the service industry. It'd been normal for most of them to sleep the day away and find a way to make money in the evening doing what they enjoyed. Jax had professed to be one of those people. The problem was Jude never could figure out exactly what he did.

Casey told Jude that Jax was a manager of a sort, for people looking for gigs in the clubs on 6th Street. Jude had had conversations with him, asking about the groups she knew, and he'd never seemed to know what she was talking about. He also hadn't known the owners or managers of many of the clubs. Jude doubted his claims and wondered if he might've been a drug dealer. The only people she had seen him talking with were other bikers.

Jude knew Jax had spent a few nights in jail and called Casey to help him find his friends to bail him out. Casey joked about it, but Jude knew she'd been embarrassed and expected more responsibility from a boyfriend. Jude had suspected it was only a matter of time before Casey would tire of his behavior.

They had been in the middle of finals. Jude had already presented the oral portion of her master's thesis and was at the apartment alone when Jax had shown up, demanding to speak with Casey. She explained that Casey had an evening exam. She could tell by the look on his face he hadn't believed her, though it was the truth. She considered Jax wouldn't know about such things because he never attended college. She wondered if he had graduated from high school.

After Jax had glanced over her shoulder into the apartment, he left. Jude could tell he was angry. It made her nervous that his bike remained parked on the street in front of their apartment building. She had continued to glance out the window and noticed he was standing on the corner, smoking a cigarette. Eventually she had heard the bike rev, and he sped away.

Jude could only think about some of the readings she'd done for one of her classes. Domestic violence and murder/suicides were most likely to occur during a break-up when one party wasn't willing to release their partner. She had been very young when it occurred in her own family.

Jude and her siblings had been separated and placed in foster care after her father, in a drunken rage, had stabbed her mother to death and then shot himself. She couldn't recall the incident, but sometimes she would be startled in her sleep by what she thought might be a gunshot. Therapists later told her this was common for people who had suffered a tragic event in childhood that they couldn't remember.

The youngest of three siblings, Jude was told her older brother and sister were placed in a group home, but she was considered adoptable. There had been an adoption placement, but for some reason it fell apart. She was told she lived with a family for six months, but she had no memory of them. By the time she left their home and returned to foster care, Jude was four.

Jude always felt she was missing something. She was certain she could find it if she could reconnect with her siblings. Her plans were to try to find them when she and Casey were back from their travels.

When Casey had returned to the apartment later that same evening, she was distracted. She had been argumentative, not her typical positive attitude. She stared off into the distance, avoided eye contact, and would force a smile that quickly faded.

Jude grew concerned as Casey moved around the apartment, beginning a task and then getting distracted by another. When Jude asked what was wrong, at first Casey said, "Nothing," but then admitted that she had talked with Jax and his obsession was worrying her. The admission meant Casey was scared.

The plan was to move out of the furnished apartment and put most of their things in storage. Casey mapped a timeline and felt they needed two months after graduation. They would be ready to leave for their backpacking adventure through Europe. When they returned to Austin after their travels, they had planned to get another apartment together, then work until they could afford their own places.

Jude thought about the times they had sat up late into the night talking about their plans. They had looked up the hostels they would stay in and had budgeted their money. Casey thought it would be fun to find jobs in some places so they could acclimate themselves into the communities and learn more about the culture.

Everything had been going as planned until Jax balked at Casey leaving Austin. Jude was under the impression that the couple had an understanding; however, Jax was much more serious about their relationship than Casey. Jax had been a controlling male who didn't want Casey to be out of his sight for any reason. It was hindering the excitement, as the time had drawn closer for them to leave.

Casey and Jude had become secretive. Casey had grown cautious of taking things to storage, worried Jax might be spying on her. Jude also suspected that Casey hadn't been honest with Jax and may have assured him that she had changed her plans.

Casey knew Jax's habits. She had told Jude one morning that Jax was probably asleep and wouldn't be likely to see them leave. "The time is now!" Casey said. "We leave today!"

Jude was startled by the sudden decision, but she didn't argue. Neither of them had much to pack. Casey had proposed they take a quick trip to Galveston to visit the beach before boarding a flight from Houston to London. She had an old compact car she planned to sell in Houston before they left. Jude hadn't questioned the decision to leave from Houston instead of Austin. In hindsight, she wondered about it.

"We had every detail planned," Jude told Birdie. "We only wanted to walk on the beach, eat some seafood, and then drive to Houston, sell the car, and take a cab to the airport." Her eyes glistened as she looked to Birdie in the lamp light.

There was a loud crash against the side of the house as the wind whipped and tore at the trees. "That's probably some debris flying around out there." Birdie got up and went to the door, looking through the slat in the shutters. As she stood at the door, watching limbs and pieces of metal fly down the street in front of the house, the lights flickered, and then everything went dark.

CHAPTER 7

BIRDIE

BIRDIE FELT HER way toward the dining room table and lit one of the oil lamps. She took it to the kitchen, then returned for candles.

"Not to worry. We have emergency lighting right here. I'm surprised we had electricity as long as we did. This area is notorious for the lights flickering off at the slightest provocation. Some of these streets flood if someone spills a drink." Birdie giggled at her own joke.

"I have a feeling you were coming to the scary part of this story, the part where Jax does something stupid. It's hard to admit I've heard this before, but I have. It repeats itself daily. I worked at the Women's Crisis Center as a volunteer. I don't have enough fingers and toes to count the similar stories I've heard."

Birdie's phone rang, the bright light of the screen startling them. Birdie looked at the number. It was Barry again. Jude could only hear Birdie's part of the conversation.

"We're just fine, Barry. Thank you for checking... Well, it's me and then there's Ollie and Jude... Yes, Barry, a friend. You've not met her. She's lovely. You'd like her... Yes, you do that. Really, we're just fine."

Birdie looked to Jude. "Honestly, he acts like I don't have a brain cell left. He's afraid as it gets later, he won't be able to get a call in. The phone has been acting up. I hope he goes to bed at some point and leaves me alone."

Jude laughed at Birdie's comments.

Birdie let Ollie out the French door so he could use the doggy door if he needed and returned to her chair. "Okay, so Jax was a controlling boyfriend, and it sounds like your friend Casey might not have told you the truth of their breakup. But you think he was threatening?"

"Yes. Now I know he was," Jude continued. "Somehow, he followed us. I suspect there was a network of his biker friends relaying messages to him. Casey never considered that, but there was always someone. Every time we stopped to go to the bathroom, or for gas, suddenly there would be a motorcycle, so I'm sure he was keeping tabs and knew exactly where Casey was.

"We were on the east side of Houston, just about to get on the interstate. I was heading to the car from the bathroom of a convenience store when someone walked up behind me and clamped their hand down over my mouth. I struggled, but he showed me he could probably snap my neck, and I went limp when he forced me into the back seat of the car. When he opened the front door on the passenger side, Casey took off, and he fell. She sped away, leaving him on the ground. I looked out the back window and watched him struggle to get up. He was making his way around the back of the store, I suspect to his bike."

Birdie was shaking her head. "You're lucky you didn't get more injuries from that, Jude."

"Well, you probably can't tell, but my lips aren't really this voluptuous. They're pretty swollen and sore. I guess that happened the day before yesterday. I'm losing track of time."

"You're right. It's past midnight now. We found you on the beach yesterday, so it would've been the previous day when you were injured."

Ollie appeared at the French door, staring at them through the glass. Birdie turned to look at him. "For the love of Pete. Look at you. He's not fond of getting his lovely hair wet." Birdie laughed out loud and Ollie cocked his head. "I would say look what the cat dragged in, but that would really piss him off," she giggled.

Birdie went into the downstairs bathroom and got a towel before opening the door for Ollie to come inside. She explained to Jude that he must have been desperate to do his business, because ordinarily he wouldn't venture out into the rain, let alone a hurricane. His predicament tickled Birdie, and she smiled at him as she rubbed his coat dry. When she was done, Ollie went to his pillow and curled up, glancing at her through his lengthy brows. Birdie got a kick out of his embarrassment. She knew he was disappointed in the change of their routine. Ordinarily, Birdie would have been in bed with a book hours ago.

Birdie returned to her chair after taking the towel to the laundry room. "He's going to be a grump as long as his schedule is different. Ollie and I are creatures of habit. However, I'm not complaining about a change of pace.

"So, there must have been an accident. Tell me more," Birdie encouraged.

"Yes, the passenger door wasn't secured, so I climbed over the seat and slammed it. If we had been smart, we would've stayed off the interstate and taken a side street or something, but I'm sure Jax had no trouble tracking us. It dawned on me later that he probably knew how to track Casey's phone. Anyway, we continued on to Galveston as we planned. We arrived in the late morning and enjoyed the beach. We went to the Strand, walked around and ate a late lunch.

"Our plan was to return to Houston in time to sell the car and get to the airport the following morning. We didn't make it to the causeway. Jax showed up out of nowhere, attempting to run Casey off the road on Harborside."

Birdie knew this obsessive, stalking behavior. She had heard it so many times before. The only thing different about Jude's story was she wasn't the love interest. She just happened to be with Casey at the time. Jude's problem had been she didn't recognize the danger when the controlling began.

"You were caught up in someone else's fixations. I'm sorry you had to experience that, Jude. You said you were the only one who survived. Does that mean Jax is deceased?"

"I don't know about him. There was another car involved. Those two people died. There were witnesses, according to the man who interviewed me, who said they saw a motorcycle speeding away. If Jax thinks Casey is still alive … I don't know what to think. I left the hospital because I really thought he would come barging in there looking for her. When I walked out, I kept looking over my shoulder." Jude had tears in her eyes. Birdie could tell by the tremble in her voice she was afraid, traumatized by the thought that Jax might still be looking for them.

"You're safe here. If that boy is out there on a motorcycle in this storm, well, he deserves what he gets."

"I feel bad about leaving Casey there, in the hospital." Jude continued to sob. "She was so beautiful. She—"

"She's not there, Jude. She's gone to a better place, better than Europe. Her spirit lives on outside the body she was just using temporarily."

Birdie was quiet for a while after that, allowing Jude to cry and feel her sadness.

Jude smiled through her tears. "She was so excited about going to Europe. We both were."

"I've been to Europe. I can tell you all about it. It's old. The buildings are, anyway. Don't get me wrong, I like old buildings. They're beautiful, and you can stand on a cobbled street and imagine the history. The churches are lovely, though there are places right here just as lovely. I know that's not helping you make a decision, but you can plan to go to Europe in the future. The immediate question is what will you do now?"

"I'll figure it out. I guess I should go back to Austin, rent an apartment and clean out the storage unit."

"That would be practical," Birdie said. "However, I've never been one for practicality. Did this Jax guy know about the storage unit?"

"Yes, he helped Casey move some stuff over there."

"Well, I'd avoid it. Did you give the police his name and other information so they could apprehend him?"

"Yes, I gave them everything I knew about him."

"You've done your part. This is what I know about death: it's not the end. For Casey, it's a new beginning. She's already into that journey and watching you. Her spirit is aware. Don't ask me how I know that, but I do. I've known about spiritual things since I was young. Casey wishes you could see what she sees. She's proud of you because she knows for a long time, you depended on her spirit to guide you." Birdie took a sip of wine and put the half full glass on the table beside her. "Casey was a mentor to you, an example of someone living their life to the fullest every day, but she was a little reckless, and she made some bad choices. That was the most important thing she's shown you. If she could talk to you right now, she would say you should learn from her mistakes in relationships and forge ahead with your own life."

"I think she just did."

"Did what?"

"She just talked to me." Jude wiped the tears from her eyes and smiled at Birdie. "I wondered why I followed you to your house this morning. Why I was so easily led by someone I didn't know. After I got here, I thought my thinking was clouded, but the truth is I have never thought so clearly in my life."

"You followed an old woman and her little dog to keep them company in the storm," Birdie laughed. "No, I know what you're saying." She held her arms out to her sides. "This whole deal is grander than a plan we could've devised, and we didn't have to stand in a gothic cathedral with a loud organ to figure it out." Birdie clapped her hands above her head. "I've got an idea, Jude. Maybe I've had a little too much wine, but I've got a notion."

Birdie left the room, collected a silver candelabra and three tall tapers. She placed it on the side table between them and lit one of the candles.

"This light represents Casey and the life shown to you through her. This is you." Birdie picked up Casey's candle and lit another. "Your light shines still. And this is me." Birdie lit her candle with Casey's. "Because of Casey, I got to know you."

Their faces were aglow with the three candles lit between them. Birdie's eyes twinkled in the light, and Jude smiled at her.

"This light, in the middle of a hurricane, was meant to be," Birdie declared. She picked up her wineglass and held it in the air. "To you, our sweet Casey, and the life you lived. Thank you for bringing Jude to me."

Jude picked up her wineglass. "To you, our sweet Birdie, and the life you showed me through Casey."

"You know, we never see things as clearly as when we can get away from them and view them from a distance. That's why I always sit in the last rows of the movie theater." Birdie took a sip of wine and winked at Jude. "I know that's silly, but it's true. It's all about perspective. I had a very good friend who taught me all about it. He could see me from a distance, and he didn't mind telling me what he saw. Trouble was I couldn't understand his perspective at the time. I had to mature a great deal before I realized what he was trying to tell me. I was dumb, as most other people. I wanted to hold a thing right up to my face and rail at it, condemn it for being so large and overwhelming. All I needed to do was hold it at arm's length, maybe set it down and walk across the room, look back at it and see how insignificant it was."

Birdie's eyes were misty, and she rubbed her lips together. She ran her fingers through her hair, then laughed and shook her finger in the air. "You know, Jude, it's not that the elderly are any wiser than anyone else. It's that they've finally set a thing down and walked across the room. When they look back at that thing, it's not what it was. Decades pass and people evolve. Those looming obstacles that hung in front of us were nothing, even though at the time, they seemed like everything."

Ollie sighed and rolled his eyes. Birdie knew he thought she was crazy most of the time, but this interruption to his routine was irritating him. And, as a superior being, he already knew all of this wisdom.

She sent him a silent message: *We're humans, Ollie. What do you expect?*

CHAPTER 8

JUDE

BY 2:00 A.M. JUDE was snuggled under expensive sheets in Birdie's guest room, thinking about the evening. She recalled sitting in the emergency room, mourning Casey, worried Jax would burst in with a weapon and threaten them all. She had been willing to cover herself with sand on the beach and let nature take its course. However, Birdie had rescued her.

An odd woman, Birdie. Maybe she's one of those occult people, a witch. She certainly has odd ideas, creates a spontaneous candle ceremony when the lights go out.

Reflecting on Birdie's tipsy talk, Jude didn't think her own situation could be anything but a looming obstacle. She failed to see how it could possibly be any less complicated given distance. She thought Birdie might've been referring to specific situations in her own past, but she hadn't elaborated. Jude was curious. There was no way for her to hold her current situation at arm's length.

She wasn't sleepy, having slept for most of the day, but she was ready to crawl in bed. She thought she could escape the constant wind whistling around the house and the pounding rain. The noise continued, a screaming, like a woman in pain. It was provoking, but somehow familiar. Jude was ready for it to cease. There were unexplained thuds and distant clanging— noises frequent enough to rouse anyone who dared to doze.

The anxiety she was feeling might be a result of the accident, Jax, and her injuries, but the wailing of the wind was also inciting her. She was thankful for Birdie's calming influence and the safety of her home.

The room was dark. Birdie had led her upstairs with an oil lamp, showing Jude where there was a flashlight in the nightstand beside the bed. They tested it, demonstrating the batteries worked. Jude pulled the drawer open and removed the light, feeling the way along the cylinder for the On button. She flicked the light on and shone the beam around the room. She looked at the books on the bookshelf. There were a variety by authors she recognized, some books she had read, others she intended to read. She moved closer, holding the light steady on a name—*Barry Barnes.*

That's Birdie's nephew. Jude looked at the title: *Reframing Loss to Define Your Future.* She moved closer to the shelf and removed the book, holding the light on the pages she flipped open. There was a lengthy note in the front of the book to Birdie from Barry, acknowledging her influence in his life and her help with coping with the loss of his parents. It brought tears to Jude's eyes. She wiped them away, thinking she didn't even know this guy. But she knew Birdie—at least, she thought she knew Birdie. She turned the book over in her hands and looked at the back cover. There was a thumbnail photo, and Jude squinted to make out the profile. From what she could see, Barry was indeed handsome as all get-out, as Birdie had said.

Jude took some time to find a way to prop the flashlight so she could use both hands to hold the book. She mounded the pillows and leaned into them, rolling on her side so the light would fall just right. Flipping past the note, Jude landed on the dedication page. The book was dedicated to Birdie. It was a beautiful dedication, again bringing Jude to tears.

What's the deal with Birdie? She speaks of this guy as if he's some kind of pest.

Jude began reading. She couldn't believe the story. Not only had Barry lost his parents when he was in college, but before that he lost his siblings in a boating accident. He was the only surviving child of three, and he had been the oldest. In high school, his best friend was electrocuted in a freak accident. He lost his parents and grandparents later. Birdie was his only living relative. By 4:00 a.m. Jude had completed the short book and held it closed in her hand with her head tilted to the ceiling.

The wind and rain continued to batter against the windows and push at the house. Jude flicked the dimming light off and put the book on the nightstand. She rolled over facing the wall of windows, knowing she should sleep. She thought of the losses in her own life. She hadn't considered them before because she never thought of her biological family as belonging to her. They were people she never knew, and what she knew of them she couldn't accept.

After Jude's first adoptive placement fell through, she must have tried not to get attached. She was too young to understand the real reasons. When she was old enough, the professionals who had arranged the placement had moved on. There was no one available to explain things to her. Other families never belonged to her. She considered them from a distance, watching to see if they were real. In her opinion, few of them ever were.

Jude was a good student. It was all she could rely on, so she decided that's what she would be. Her social life in high school was pitiful. She hesitated to accept a date because of the explanations she would have to make about her family. It was too cumbersome. With the burden of secondhand clothing and less-than-fashionable haircuts, the thought of explanations was just too much. There was no one at that time she considered a friend.

In hindsight, she regretted not being more outgoing. She had never allowed herself to be vulnerable or share her burden with anyone. Now she could see how that might have made a difference.

It was history. There was nothing Jude could do about it, but she chastised herself regardless. Maybe she could just take control of her life now. Maybe that's what the accident and Casey's death was for—to show her she could be in control of something. She would be forced to make her own decisions and think for herself.

Lightning flashed outside, and Jude watched it through the small holes in the shutters. Strange shadows danced on the wall in the unpredictable flashes. She was in a strange bed yet again, a reminder of those nights in her childhood when things were foreign and dark. It seemed surreal, but for the first time, she felt she was where she belonged. It was comfortable. She didn't have to listen to sounds in the hall before getting up to go to the bathroom. She was confident she could go to the kitchen and help herself to anything from the refrigerator. Birdie had given her that permission. Jude trusted it was true.

She'd moved through her childhood alone, but it was different because others always made decisions for her. She didn't have to come up with a plan; the adults prescribed what would happen, and she had no input. If there was anything to be grateful for, it was that Jude could make her own plan, and it could be exactly what she wanted. She told herself she didn't have to figure it out. She would wait out the storm.

The ceremony Birdie initiated was a closure of sorts, but it was also a new beginning, a rebirth. She wasn't alone; Birdie was downstairs, and somehow that was all she had and all she needed. If she thought too long about it, she might convince herself otherwise, so Jude closed her eyes.

CHAPTER 9

BIRDIE

THE WIND WAS more violent than Birdie cared to admit. She had peeked out the slats of the shutters on the front door before going to her room. She trusted Jude would be able to negotiate the upstairs with the flashlight she had shown her. The oil lamps made her nervous, and Birdie didn't like walking around the house with a flame fueled by liquid. She found her own flashlight and lowered the wick on the lamp, extinguishing the flame.

Ollie followed Birdie into her room and settled himself on his pillow. Birdie waited until he was out of the way before going into her closet for her gown and robe. She felt in the dark for the hook. As she folded her jeans and tunic, she thought about Jude's predicament.

Barry might not like it, but Birdie was more than willing for Jude to remain with her until she had recuperated and made a decision about the next step in her life. She had a good feeling about Jude. She reminded Birdie of herself at that age, a little isolated, insecure about her next steps. It was obvious to Birdie that Casey had been Jude's crutch, the extrovert daredevil that Jude was not. While Jude might have admired Casey's devil-may-care attitude, it certainly proved to be dangerous and, in the end, fatal.

Her words about perspective and distance made Birdie think about seeing herself in Jude. She would never have been able to view herself as a young woman when she was one. There were too many things in her way, one of which was herself. Henry was right about that. She was her biggest obstacle.

Birdie took a sip of the water from the decanter on her bedside table. She tilted her head as she swallowed and wondered why she cared what Barry thought about her decisions. She closed her eyes and fought not to give in to the lump in her throat. She knew why she cared. Their family had endured loss, more loss than Barry should've had to shoulder at a young age. While his clinging behavior irritated her at times, she knew if he was not so attentive, she would miss him more than she could imagine. He was a son to her, and she was his only parent figure. She knew he was desperate to keep her, almost frantic. He was not as resolved as she was to the notion that all things must die. She feared him standing by her deathbed, begging her not to leave him.

Why she could see the answer to Jude's dilemma so clearly and had such trouble figuring out her own life. Birdie hit her pillow with her fist, plumping it. Ollie glanced at her. "Good night, old boy," Birdie said. "Sweet dreams." Ollie huffed, resting his head on his paws. Birdie gave a little giggle. She was always comforted by the fact that she and Ollie knew each other so well. They tolerated each other's quirks. It amused her that Ollie didn't seem nearly as entertained about it as she was. He was her captive audience, but she didn't think he'd have it any other way.

Normally, Birdie would read a chapter or two before going to sleep, but the lack of electricity presented a problem. It had been a long day, emotionally, and physically draining. She had planned breakfast before leaving the kitchen for the night. The coffee pot might be an issue with no electricity. She had covered the cinnamon rolls with plastic wrap and left them on the counter.

Her phone lit up and Birdie glanced toward it, wondering what was going on. She knew from the symbol that it was a text, but she didn't normally do that. *Barry?* Surely he didn't expect her to respond at such a ridiculous hour. She decided to ignore it. Her finger hovered over the symbol, but she couldn't bring herself to touch it.

Why Barry's attention irritate her. It wasn't that she didn't appreciate that he cared. That wasn't it. It was that he made her feel like she was incompetent. She wasn't. She was capable of using good judgment and making decisions. He encouraged her to move to an independent apartment closer to him. She argued it would be closer to him but away from her friends, neighbors, and the house she loved. And what about Ollie? The apartment complex wouldn't allow dogs. She refused. Maybe if she was a fumbling old woman unable to find her way to the market, but she wasn't.

She reached for the phone, held her finger over the text symbol, and read it. *Worried about you! Call me when you get up in the morning and let me know you're okay.*

Birdie smiled to herself and hit the respond symbol. *I'm wonderful. Ollie and I found a mermaid on the beach this morning, and we've been drinking wine and singing songs as the storm rages on. Love you Barry. LOL*

She decided to add the 'lol' so Barry would know it was a joke. It was an afterthought. She really intended for him to believe she was out of her mind, thinking she found a mermaid. At some point she would have to tell him she was planning on going on a cruise with her mah-jongg group. They had been talking about it for over a year, and finally they had made the reservations. They were going shopping the following week for new outfits.

Birdie feared telling Barry because he might not think she should go. She didn't want to hear that. She'd rather spring it on him at the last minute. There were still a few details to work out, like boarding Ollie, but she could deal with that. For now, she would focus on assisting Jude with her plans; then she would tackle a conversation with Barry about her desire for travel.

As soon as she settled in, comfortable enough to fall asleep, the tingling in her legs began to distract her. Birdie moved her legs, wadding her nightgown between them to cushion them. They didn't hurt, they pulsed. It was a constant thrumming of nothing, but it was enough to drive her batty when she wanted to sleep.

"Oh, for heaven's sake." Birdie threw back the covers and made her way to the bathroom, feeling her way around furniture and the door frame. She located the medicine cabinet and tried to avoid the metallic squeak as she eased it open. She felt along the second shelf and found the bottle that she was sure contained the aspirin she hoped would remove the pulsing from her legs. She decided to take three tablets for extra measure, placing the bottle on the edge of the sink.

Birdie made her way back to the bed and took a long sip of water. She glanced at her phone, thinking she should plug it in, then realized there was no electricity and that would be useless. She didn't need to bother with feeling her way along the wall for the outlet.

Sleep came, slithering across the linen pillowcase and wrapping her in a foggy fantasy. Henry was there. They walked on the beach, their bikes parked near the rock groin, his calming voice answering her worried anxiety and fretful concerns. Weathered men in tattered clothing passed them, giving no notice. Some of them had scruffy dogs to keep them company. Birdie noticed the mongrels, admiring their adaptation to the nomadic life of their companions. Wandering between 18th Street and 34th, the men drifted from the seawall to Broadway, picking up discarded food containers and bits of objects.

Henry didn't mention the men, if he noticed. Somehow he was back—different, but back—allowing her to be the level head. Birdie smiled in her dream; no one had ever referred to her as a level head. It had always been Henry offering her a calm word to settle her down, his even, lilting voice beckoning her to relax and think through any concerns.

In her dream, she knew Henry wasn't there, but there was something about the way he was allowing her to guide him, something unfamiliar but validating. She wanted to remember that feeling.

CHAPTER 10

JUDE

THE AROMA WAFTED upstairs from the kitchen below. Jude rolled over in bed, once again aware she was in a strange room. The rain continued to fall, but it didn't sound as windy. She stretched, then went to the window to peer through the slats. The rain now fell from above, not blowing sideways as it had the previous day. It wasn't the frantic whipping that pounded at the house the previous evening.

There was enough light coming through the windows to see her way into the bathroom. Jude brushed her teeth and dressed, then went down the back stairs. She realized the coffee pot was brewing, so the electricity must be on. She flicked a switch and sure enough, the power had been restored. She couldn't think about what had to happen for the timer on the pot to come on in time for her morning cup.

Birdie was nowhere to be seen, but Ollie was standing by the back door. Jude opened it for Ollie, and he walked across the porch and out the doggie door. She went back to the coffee pot and poured herself a cup, then walked to the porch to wait for Ollie. Jude decided to peek into Birdie's room. She glimpsed her sleeping on her side. She walked to the bed to make sure Birdie was breathing. She was. *She must be really tired.* It was late in the morning.

Recalling Birdie's routine from the first day they met, Jude went to Ollie's food and replenished his bowl, then filled his water bowl. She looked out the front door and saw the newspaper wrapped in plastic on the sidewalk. Jude took an umbrella from the rack in the vestibule and walked down the sidewalk to retrieve the paper, fighting the umbrella in the wind. She let Ollie back in and went to get a second cup of coffee. She took two cinnamon rolls before settling down with the newspaper.

Jude read through the paper, then washed the dishes she used. She paced, wondering when Birdie would appear. She was beginning to get concerned. Ollie had settled on his pillow in Birdie's room. Jude talked aloud to Ollie, hoping it would cause Birdie to stir, but nothing. She approached the bed again and noted Birdie was still breathing.

Birdie's phone rang. It startled Jude and she jumped and glanced down to see Barry's name. Birdie didn't budge.

"Hello," Jude said into Birdie's phone.

"Who is this?" Barry asked.

"This is Jude. I'm here with Birdie. I stayed with her during the storm. She's still asleep."

"Well, okay. This is Barry. I asked her to call me this morning, and I assumed that would be a couple of hours ago. I was getting worried. I've never known Birdie to sleep this late."

"I came into her room to check on her. I've been up a while and nothing I've done has roused her. I'm standing right by her bed now, and she hasn't moved. She's breathing normally."

"Did she take anything, like a sleeping pill or something?"

"I don't know. There's nothing here on her nightstand. We have electricity now. It was out for a few hours last night. Let me look in the bathroom. Oh, there is a bottle here. It's a prescription from a Dr. Calder for Vicodin for pain."

"That's her dentist. Has she been to the dentist?"

"No, not since I've been here. Wait, the date for this is two years ago."

"How many pills was the prescription for?"

"Ten. There are seven in the bottle now, so she could have taken one or maybe three."

"Well, that doesn't sound like it would be lethal or anything. Birdie doesn't like to take medicine. She never has, so a painkiller would probably make her very sleepy. I can come down and be there by late tomorrow."

"That's not necessary. I know Birdie would love to see you, but I'll be here with her until she wakes up for sure."

"Well, okay. How long are you planning to stay? I've never heard her mention your name before."

"We only recently met, and she was nice enough to let me stay during the storm. When she wakes, I'll talk with her about my plans. I got caught here in Galveston without transportation, and Birdie has been very nice."

"What's your name again?"

"Judith Reynolds."

"And you don't have a car or anything?"

"No. I was with a friend and we had an accident. The car was taken by a wrecker."

"And where's your friend?"

"At the hospital."

"Hmm, I see. Okay, well, I'll say goodbye."

He hung up. Jude knew it sounded strange. She didn't want him to be concerned, but she didn't know what she could say to make him feel better. He didn't know her, and he had no reason to trust her.

88

She put her hand on Birdie's forehead. It was cool to the touch, not feverish. She shook Birdie gently with her hand on her shoulder, but Birdie just took a deep breath and continued to sleep.

Jude went back to the den and picked up the newspaper, turning to the puzzle page. She got another cup of coffee and found a pen on Birdie's kitchen counter. She sat in her favorite chair and began to work the puzzles. Ollie wandered into the den and stood at the back door. Jude got up to let him out and noticed an hour had gone by.

There was a frantic knock at the front door. Jude opened the door to two people under a black umbrella, an older woman with pink sponge rollers wound in her hair and a bald man with thick black glasses. They stared at her with wide eyes, saying nothing.

"Yes?" Jude said.

"Well, say something, Wendell," the woman said.

Wendell looked to the woman with the rollers in her hair. "I'm thinking, Velma."

"You've had time to think all the way over here. Now say something."

Wendell cleared his throat. Jude thought they looked like cartoon characters. The woman wore a tropical print house dress and had taken the time to paint her mouth with bright red lipstick. The color was running into the rivulets surrounding her lips. Wendell—*ah, Wendell the impotent*—was peering at Jude through the rain droplets coating his glasses. He tilted his head back as if that gave him a better view. These were Birdie's neighbors, the people Birdie might have spent the hurricane with had she not been there.

"Would you like to come in?" Jude asked.

"Yes, yes we would," Velma said. "We need to see Birdie."

"Birdie is still asleep. We had a long night, and I think she might be catching up on her rest."

"Well, we need to see her," Velma insisted.

"Uh, I'm sure she will be happy to give you a call when she wakes. I'm—"

"We have to see her. Barry was clear," Wendell began.

"You've talked with Barry? Oh, I see. He must have called you after I talked with him." Jude left the door open and walked toward the back of the house. Velma and Wendell shuffled in behind her, leaving the umbrella open on the porch.

"Maybe we should just go ahead and call the police," Velma said in a high, screeching voice. Jude noted that her eyes were darting around the room. She was wringing her hands. "Wendell, I think that's what we should do. Go ahead and call the police."

Wendell shot Velma a look, frowning and then staring at the floor. Jude wondered what Barry might have told them. *Is he concerned that I'm an intruder?*

Jude took a deep breath. She wanted to figure out what their concern was. She also had some concern that Birdie had taken too much medication and was apparently sleeping it off, but she saw no need to involve law enforcement. "Maybe you two can help me rouse Birdie. I would like her to explain why she might have had the need to take some medicine during the night. It might be what's making her drowsy. Maybe if I put a damp cloth on her face? I've been hesitant to insist she wake up." Jude tried to keep her voice low and calming.

"I want to see her," Velma said, her voice still at the screech level.

"Now, Velma, just wait a minute." Wendell grabbed her arm and raised his voice. She turned to him and they began yelling at each other.

Jude sighed and watched.

CHAPTER 11

BIRDIE

"*WHAT THE HELL* is going on out here?" Birdie stood in the door to the hall. Her hair was disheveled, and she was slipping an arm into her robe. "For heaven's sake, you two could wake the dead."

"Oh, Birdie. We're so glad to see you're okay," Velma said, tears in her eyes.

"Of course I'm okay. I would be better if I could wake up to a calm, quiet house. Now what's this commotion about?" Birdie glanced around the room. "What are you two doing here, anyway? Velma, you look like hell. I've never in my life seen you leave the house looking like that."

Velma stood taller and put her hand to the rollers in her hair. She pursed her lips, calling attention to her red mouth. "We left the house in a hurry. It was an emergency."

"What's the emergency?" Birdie asked, her eyes round and wide.

"Well dammit, Birdie, you were the emergency."

"Me? How in the world could I have been the emergency? All I've been doing is sleeping." Birdie shook her head, chuckling.

Wendell paced. Jude looked to Birdie. "Maybe I can help explain." She told Birdie about waking up to find the coffee pot going and the electricity on. She told her about taking Ollie out, Barry's phone call, and her attempts to rouse Birdie from sleep. She said she found the pills beside the sink in the bathroom and assumed Birdie had taken some.

"I took aspirin during the night. My restless legs were bothering me, so I got up and took aspirin."

Jude held a finger in the air. "I'll show you what I found." She left the room and returned with the pill bottle she'd left by the sink. Birdie held her hand to her mouth, staring at the bottle.

"It was dark, the electricity was off, and I just felt inside the cabinet for the aspirin. I had no intention of taking this. I didn't use these when they were prescribed. So what time is it?"

"It's almost 2 in the afternoon. You've been asleep all this time," Jude said.

"Oh my word. I've never slept this late. I've missed half the day." She turned to Velma and Wendell. "That doesn't explain what you're doing here fighting and yelling at each other."

"Now, Birdie, we meant well. Barry called and wanted us to come and check on you. He said there was a strange woman here with you, and she wouldn't let you talk with him. He was only concerned for your welfare," Velma said.

Birdie threw her head back. "My welfare? This is my friend, Jude, by the way. You two and Barry have been very rude. I need some coffee." Birdie walked toward the kitchen.

"I'll make another pot, Birdie." Jude followed close behind her. "Have a seat. We can have a little brunch with your neighbors."

Velma's head was bent slightly after Birdie's reprimand. She peered at Jude from lowered lids. Wendell stood with his hands clasped in front of him, swaying. Birdie followed Jude and took a seat at the kitchen table. She ran her hands through her hair and yawned.

"I do feel like I'm in a fog," Birdie admitted. "That was so silly of me not to take the flashlight into the bathroom and make sure I was taking the right pills. That's a lesson learned." Birdie waved her hand in the air, raising her eyebrows to Velma, then crossed her arms in front of her. "I did want you two to meet Jude, but not under these circumstances.

Jude set a plate of cinnamon rolls on the table and poured coffee for everyone as they sat around talking about the storm. Jude suggested Birdie call Barry and let him know she was okay. Velma nodded vigorously. Wendell continued to sit quietly.

"I'm mad at him right now, Jude. He's caused this whole misunderstanding, butting into my business."

Velma's face fell and she gave Wendell a quick glance.

"He was only concerned about you. I talked with him and could tell by his voice. He only has your best interest in his heart," Jude said. "I can understand why he would be worried. I thought it sounded fishy to me while I was talking with him, and I knew he must be thinking the same thing."

"She's right," Velma said. "You need to give Barry a break. He's always cared for you, Birdie, and most of us would love to have someone that attentive to us. He was at a disadvantage being so far away and unable to monitor how you were doing during the storm. I think if he had met Jude, he would've been much relieved to know she was here with you. I'm certainly reassured and very happy to know you, Jude."

Jude nodded and smiled at Velma, trying not to stare at the color from her lips bleeding down her chin.

"You're right. I'll give him a call."

Jude watched as Wendell and Velma held onto each other as they went down the steps. The sun was breaking through, and they no longer needed the umbrella. Birdie was on the phone talking to Barry when she returned to the kitchen.

"I know. I've learned my lesson. That was certainly all my fault, but I'm so glad Jude was here to point it out to me, and she took good care of Ollie while I slept the morning away… Yes, you'll meet her. She's going to be here for a while."

Jude cleaned the kitchen while Birdie continued to talk with Barry. When she hung up, Jude turned to her and said, "I don't think I'll be here long enough to meet Barry, Birdie. I need to get back to my own life."

"Now, Jude, you know as well as I do that your own life is not well defined at the moment. I had a wonderful dream last night. My old friend was there. I haven't seen him in ages. I think it was a wonderful sign, a sign meant to tell me I'm supposed to help you. I don't often get to be the one to keep my cool, Jude. Please let me do it when I can."

"I don't know what any of that means, Birdie."

"That's because you're not thinking straight. You need me to help you get some perspective."

Jude laughed. "You have been very helpful, Birdie, and I do appreciate everything you've done for me."

Jude was not the one who took the wrong medication during the night. Birdie's insistence that she could be the one with perspective was not exactly something she professed with great conviction; however, she wanted the opportunity to prove herself.

"I know you're right, Birdie. I should take a little time to make a plan," Jude said. "My problem is I'm not sure where to start."

"That's where I come in. You have every reason to be in shock from the loss of your friend. That's understood. Give yourself permission to be in that place and give yourself some time. What better place to spend a little time than here on this island with me?" Birdie winked, hoping she had enticed Jude to stay with her a while longer. There was something about the girl she just couldn't release.

CHAPTER 12

JUDE

WHILE BIRDIE WAS in the shower, Don Roberts arrived to raise the storm blinds. The house was again filled with light. He made quick work of the chore and was gone before Birdie appeared. Jude let Ollie out and began picking up debris in the yard. She swept the porch and wiped leaves and dirt from the pots, arranging the pillows on the furniture so they could dry.

"I still feel like I have cobwebs in my brain," Birdie said as she emerged from the house. "That's why I never take that stuff when the doctors give it to me. It makes me goofy. I'm certainly sorry you had to meet Velma and Wendell like that. Trust me, they aren't fun when they've made themselves presentable, but that spectacle this morning will put you off your oatmeal."

Jude laughed. "I was distracted by her lipstick."

"Isn't that the truth? She couldn't have painted all those little cracks if she'd tried." Birdie grabbed Jude's arm to steady herself as she laughed. "We're going to Hell for laughing about that. It's shallow and mean, but so funny. I bet she let Wendell have it when she got home and looked in the mirror. Bless her heart."

A motorcycle turned the corner and rocketed down the street. Jude froze, backing herself against the house. Her heart raced and she squeezed Birdie's hand.

"Oh, child, you're still thinking about that terrible man."

Jude exhaled. "It's just that certain sounds make me jump, especially that one."

"Let's busy ourselves with something to take your mind off it. You need some clothes. Where do you think your things ended up?"

"I guess my backpack was still in the car when it was towed. My laptop is in there, too. I thought about it briefly, but I just assumed it was gone for good."

"I know someone who might be able to help. I'll make some phone calls. If we can get your backpack, that'd be nice, don't you think? I couldn't bother my friend during the storm, but I can call him now."

"For sure. That would be a great relief. There's money and other things I'd like to get back."

"Well, that's where we'll start, retrieving your belongings." Birdie walked with purpose back inside the house. She phoned an acquaintance with the police department and was able to locate both Jude's and Casey's backpacks. Jude had to answer some questions about the contents to verify she was indeed the owner. They also agreed to give her Casey's belongings after she confirmed some of the contents and mentioned she was deceased. After being placed on hold for a few minutes, a woman came back to the phone and confirmed everything could be released to Jude.

"I can't believe the officer is going to deliver them here." Jude said. "That's very accommodating." They sat with cups of coffee on the screened porch as Ollie sniffed out new smells left by the storm.

"It pays to live in one place all your life. I went to high school with Eldon. He's one of the nicest men I know, would give you the shirt off his back. He owes me nothing, but I have a soft spot for his children, and he knows it. Eldon and I went through some times. We sure did." Birdie got a faraway look, her eyes focused on nothing, a little teary. She seemed lost in her thoughts. Jude sat quiet until Birdie lifted her head and took a deep breath.

"We survived the storm, Jude. So, what's our next adventure?"

"As soon as I get my things I can be on my way. I'll see about getting a car to the airport and making my way back to Austin. I'll get an apartment and start looking for work."

"So, that's a plan," Birdie agreed. "You have a group of friends there who will be supportive and assist you with finding a place to live and maybe give you some leads on jobs?"

"I'm afraid my only real friend was Casey. I have acquaintances, but I wouldn't burden them with assisting me, and I'd probably have to keep out of the places I know Jax might be, if he's still around. I'll figure that out when I get there."

"Just consider this. I'm going to put it out there and you can decide." Birdie put her finger to her lips and raised her eyebrows, then began to smile. "I have a lengthy trip coming up with my mah-jongg group. We're cruising from here to Florida and around the Caribbean. This is selfish, mind you. I need someone to care for Ollie. I thought about boarding him, but I always worry about that. He's set in his ways, just like me. I also need someone to water my plants, pick up the newspaper, and keep an eye on the house. I guess you can see my hesitancy about asking Velma to do that?" Birdie giggled.

"This trip begins in a couple of weeks. I would be much relieved if you would consider being my house sitter. I'd be willing to compensate you and you could stay here, enjoy the beach, and take time to contemplate your next steps. In the meantime, I'd enjoy your company. You can help me decide what to pack."

Jude nodded as she listened. Birdie patted Jude's arm as she went to the kitchen. What Birdie was proposing sounded appealing. It would certainly give her time to think. Maybe she thought too much. Casey always said she did. While she was contemplating the pros and cons, worried about what someone would think, the opportunity would pass her by.

Jude had considered seeking jobs she could do virtually. She could actually live anywhere, but that might be a cop-out for her and feeding into her fears of facing people on a daily basis. It was something Casey was always hounding her about, telling her she needed to practice meeting people face-to-face and getting to know them. She realized what Birdie was offering might be the time she needed to rethink her plans, an opportunity to adjust to losing Casey. It made sense to her to allow herself the time and not rush into any decisions. Maybe she didn't need to go back to Austin. Maybe there were other places she should consider. She would not have to try to avoid Jax if she didn't go back.

Ollie approached Jude, laying his head on her knee. She rubbed him behind the ears. They were forming a bond. He was so much easier than a human. She didn't want to think of him boarded with strange people while Birdie traveled. As Jude picked up the empty coffee cup to head to the kitchen, she thought she might have made a decision.

"Thanks for having trust in me, Birdie," Jude said, "but we've only known each other a few days. Don't you think you should run this house-sitting idea by Barry? I would feel very awkward being here without his approval."

Birdie clucked her tongue and shook her head. "He's made you feel uncomfortable about being here, and that makes me mad."

"Oh, Birdie, don't be mad at him. He can't make me feel one way or the other. Those feelings stem from growing up in other people's houses. If I feel uncomfortable, that's more about me than it is him. You have to ask yourself why I don't have any friends in Austin. I know that's my fault, not anyone else. I can't put myself out there. Socially, I'm a dud. That's why this offer sounds so attractive. It gives me a place to hide. So, instinctively, that should raise a flag and tell me it's the wrong thing to do. That's what Casey would say."

"Casey, may she rest in peace, sounded like a wild child to me, your polar opposite. You're a shy girl, aren't you?" Birdie said as she moved around the kitchen putting things away. She wiped the counter and looked up at Jude with one hand on her hip. "There's nothing wrong with being a little leery of people. Some of them can be disappointing, as you well know.

"You're a self-starter, Jude. You've demonstrated that to me many times during this short stay. I trust you and was so lucky to have you with me overnight. I'm grateful for that. What you've shared about yourself and Casey tells me you have an instinct. You were the one, of the two of you, who knew to be suspicious of Jax. You were the one with a head on your shoulders—"

There was a knock at the front door. Jude remained seated at the table while Birdie went to answer.

"Well, that was mighty fast. Come on in here. I want you to meet somebody."

CHAPTER 13

BIRDIE

JUDE ENTERED THE den to meet Birdie and a very tall black man in a dark suit carrying Jude's backpack. He was a nice-looking man with close-cropped graying hair. His smile was wide, and his eyes twinkled when he looked to Jude.

"Jude, this is my dear friend Eldon Reed. We've been friends since God was a child. Eldon, say hello to my new friend Jude. She spent the hurricane with me."

"Glad to meet you, Jude." Eldon extended his free hand to shake hers. His hand was warm and smooth. "I'm sorry you were one of the people in that tragic accident.

"Thank you for bringing this," Jude said. "I was afraid it might be gone forever. I appreciate it. I guess I was the lucky one."

"No problem. Any friend of Birdie's is a friend of mine. Happy to help."

"Can I offer you some coffee, Eldon?" Birdie said.

"No, I can't stay. Just on my way to Pete Hanson's service."

"That's right. I was sorry to hear about Pete," Birdie said.

Eldon left, telling Birdie to call him if she ever needed anything. She stood at the front door and watched him until he got in his car. "Casey's backpack is in here on the floor, Jude. It's heavy. I can't lift it."

Jude walked to the door and looked at the backpack. It was indeed Casey's. "I'll move it somewhere. Where should I put it?"

"Don't worry about it now. We'll figure that out later." Birdie waved her hand in the air, dismissing a need to deal with Casey's heavy bag. She walked toward the kitchen. "I'm off my routine. This day started off so strange, I don't even know what day it is. How about a walk on the beach, Jude? Ollie and I have missed at least a day, if I'm not mistaken."

Ollie perked up when he saw Birdie taking his leash off the hook in the vestibule. He cantered across the porch and down the steps, well ahead of Birdie and Jude. They walked quietly for a few blocks, and then Birdie began pointing out houses, talking about the people she had known who had lived in them.

She knew the histories and shared memories of playing with children living there when she was growing up.

"This street was full of kids. We rode bikes and skated the full length of the street with no worries from our parents. The front doors were always unlocked, and there was no air conditioning. You could hear people talking, phones ringing, babies crying, and dog's barking inside the houses through the screened doors."

Birdie giggled. "We had a big Collie. She was the sweetest thing, Brenda. She was afraid of thunder. Shook like a leaf when a storm would blow in. The Stubblefields lived in that house to the right of mine. They were nice people and knew Brenda was afraid of thunder. She slept out on the back porch at night. Mama never was wild about having an inside dog.

"One night, after everyone was asleep, a storm blew in and apparently there was some thunder. The next morning, here comes Mrs. Stubblefield with Brenda in tow. She proceeds to tell Mama that during the night, Brenda opened their back screen door and came inside. She stood between the twin beds Mr. and Mrs. Stubblefield slept in and shook, spraying both of them with rainwater from her coat. They let her sleep the rest of the night on the floor between their beds."

Jude laughed, visualizing a big Collie entering someone's bedroom during the night and doing such a thing. "What did your mother say?"

"She was so embarrassed. I knew she was beside herself because the skin on her neck and chest turned a bright red. I can still remember the printed house dress she wore. That blush on her chest matched the bright pink flower on the fabric. She stared at Mrs. Stubblefield with big eyes, unable to say anything. I watched, thinking Mama might pass out. Mrs. Stubblefield knew Mama was caught off guard and said they didn't mind letting Brenda spend the night, but I bet they latched their screen door after that.

"Mama baked them a pie and sent them a flower arrangement. Daddy thought it was the funniest thing he'd ever heard, but Mama never laughed about it. She hung her head when it was mentioned, and that pink rash crawled up her chest."

Birdie muttered to herself about not knowing what happened to the family. She had lost track of them after they moved away.

As they approached the intersection to the seawall, Birdie waved to a bicycle vendor and called out to him.

"Afternoon, Birdie. Have a nice walk," he called back.

Birdie allowed Ollie off his leash when they got to the beach. He chased seagulls and stood with his nose pointing toward the water, allowing his long scruffy hair to blow in the wind.

As they stood side by side watching Ollie, Birdie said, "I was thinking it's easy for me to know these people in my neighborhood. I've seen them most of the days of my life. Before me, they knew my parents. There was no risk to knowing them. They were just there. It's different for you, Jude. You've lived so many places, with the foster care and all. That had to be hard for a kid, but you've graduated with an advanced degree. I admire that. I truly do."

Jude's gaze was on the surf. Birdie thought she might have embarrassed her by speaking about her past. She called out to Ollie, approaching him to reattach his leash. As she returned to the spot they were standing, Birdie noticed Jude had tears in her eyes.

"I'm sorry, Jude, I didn't mean to make you cry."

"No, Birdie, it's okay. No one—and I mean no one, ever—has told me they admired me for anything. That just hit me. It's sad, but it's also so nice to hear, finally." The tears were rolling down Jude's face. "I know I'm blubbering. I'm sorry. I'll get myself together. Don't say anything else, Birdie. No more mushy talk. I can't take it." Jude was laughing through her tears.

Birdie was saddened by what Jude told her. To think a person made it to adulthood without ever being told they were loved, appreciated, or admired. It made her reflect on her own upbringing and how many times she was embraced and praised. She thought about Barry when he was a child and how she was constantly hugging him and his siblings, telling him how proud she was of him. She recalled sitting in the bleachers during his basketball games, cheering for him, and going to his award assemblies. She was aware there were children there with no family support, and it plucked at her heartstrings. Now here stood Jude, a grown-up product of that neglect.

Birdie glanced at the debris on the beach. The tide must have been higher than normal with storm surge during the night. There was driftwood and other vestiges littering the beach, and they had to negotiate around a large storage tank covered with barnacles. Birdie would monitor the beach and call the city if she needed to make sure they were aware of the debris. She told Jude she probably wouldn't have to make the call. "They're usually prompt about tending to the beach after a storm.

"Is there a dress or something in that backpack of yours?" Birdie asked.

"Yes, there is. Why, are you tired of seeing me in the same clothes every day?" Jude grinned, wiping tears from her cheeks.

"No, you always look nice. I was just thinking it might be nice to get out of the house and go out to eat this evening. Today's Thursday, the snapper special tonight at the Club. It's a quiet place with good food and service, just for members, but they're strict about dress. It's an old family membership, not my idea, but comfortable and good food. It's quiet, so people can carry on a conversation without talking over loud music and dishes clattering."

"Oh, Birdie, that sounds expensive. I feel like you think you need to entertain me and you don't. I'm happy with a peanut butter and jelly sandwich, really."

"I could be happy with that most of the time also, but we've been in the house all this time behind those shutters. I'm stir-crazy, and I want to get dressed sometimes and go out. You can humor an old woman, can't you? We can have peanut butter and jelly tomorrow."

"Okay. It might be nice to get out. I'll probably need to iron my sundress."

"Great, I'll call Dennis when we get home and let him know we're coming. You know, during the storm, when it was raining and my routine was altered, I was thinking. I imagine rainy days are for pondering. We're supposed to slow down and think through the things we've been neglecting, the things that shouldn't be dealt with in a knee jerk. Maybe that's what we're supposed to do during the hurricane. Maybe everyone was given the opportunity to consider their lives, think about their next steps, reflect on how far they've come. Rainy days knock us off-kilter, storm into our lives, and wash the mustiness away. I don't regret them. I surely don't."

As they walked toward the house, Birdie reflected on the words she had said to Jude. It was true. The storm had given her an opportunity to be shuttered in with Jude and think about her life by reflecting on someone else's. They were different, the two of them, as different as they could be, but they seemed to have the same insecurities. It reminded her of herself and Henry.

CHAPTER 14

JUDE

AS JUDE SLIPPED into the freshly pressed sundress, she looked to the nightstand for her earrings, silver hoops she wore with everything. She secured them into her pierced ears and noted the book she'd read during the peak of the storm. She remembered the feeling it gave her—a recognition that she too needed to communicate with others, be more open about herself, be authentic.

Birdie had been right. Jude aligned herself with Casey so she didn't have to make decisions or commit. She followed Casey and did everything recommended to her. It seemed safe at the time, but in reality it was the worst thing she could've done, and in the end, it was denial of herself. She made up her mind that following Casey's plan was no longer viable for her. She was tempted to return to the familiar, but Birdie's house was comfortable and felt safe. But was it too safe? *How do people make these decisions?*

Jude dug in her bag for a silver bracelet and her watch. She slipped them on and took fifty dollars from a side pocket to put in her purse. Twisting her hair into a loose knot at her neck, she fluffed the tendrils down each side of her face. Jude grabbed a lightweight cardigan and headed downstairs after slipping on a pair of tan sandals.

Ollie stood when Jude entered the room. Birdie was seated in her favorite chair, looking at the newspaper. "Well, look at you. I still recognize you, lovely as ever, but you clean up real nice. I'm glad you brought a sweater. It can get a little cool in that building in the evening."

Birdie drove them fifteen blocks to the Club, parking in the back where there were only four other cars. It was an elegant and understated setting. The back of the building was all glass, facing a tropically landscaped courtyard and pool. Birdie was greeted with hugs, and they were led to a sitting area facing the courtyard. Birdie ordered a martini and asked Jude to order whatever she wanted.

"I'll have chardonnay."

When the waiter left, Jude commented that it was a lovely building.

"It's been here forever—as long as I've been around, anyway. I can't tell you the history. I'm not much on paying attention to those things. My parents were devastated when I refused to make my debut." Birdie rolled her eyes, her voice cracking. "It would've been a farce, me in a white gown, bowing and smiling like I approved of such things. Don't get me started on that. Let's just say people will walk in and wave, but I'm more tempted to want to shoot the finger." Birdie giggled. "One of these days, when I've had three martinis, I'll tell you all about it, but that won't be today."

Jude smiled at Birdie. She was sure there were many things she hadn't discovered about this woman, and she was inclined to stick around and figure Birdie out. But she was just as desperate to figure out her own life.

Drinks were served, along with cheese straws and grapes. Jude accepted the wine and sat back in the comfortable chair, wondering how a planned adventure with Casey in Europe had turned into sipping cocktails with this older woman in a private club on a secluded, shaded boulevard in Galveston. She watched a couple of squirrels running between two large oak trees in the courtyard.

"Hey, Jude." Birdie laughed. "I told you I was going to do that. We can sit out there under that oak canopy and have our dinner, if you'd like. I can ask Dennis about the mosquito situation."

"That sounds nice. I'll leave it up to you. It looks beautiful."

Birdie stood and walked toward the bar in the next room. Jude glanced at another group across the large common area. They were visiting in hushed voices, occasionally laughing loudly. She slipped her arms into the sleeves of the cardigan.

"Dennis says it's been pleasant out by the pool and he recommends dining there tonight. He says to take advantage now before the mosquitoes have a chance to hatch since the rain from the storm. I went ahead and ordered for us. Follow me. They'll bring our drinks out."

Jude stood and followed Birdie, a waiter holding the door as they walked out onto a tiled patio. It was pleasant, the weather having turned less humid following the storm. Birdie led Jude to a table with comfortable chairs. A string of white lights flickered on above their heads.

"This would be a great place for a party," Jude commented.

"Oh, this is the scene of well-appointed celebrations many times during the year. People here don't miss an opportunity to throw a party. It's a three-tux town." Birdie winked, shifting in her seat to stare back through the glass wall into the building. "My closet used to be full of cocktail dresses and formals. All the women have such things, and seamstresses to alter their

116

appearance so they can reinvent them for a second showing. Our closets bulged with sequins and feathers. Mother was a frequent customer of the shoe shop on 21st. Mr. Ruiz dyed her satin shoes several times, tinting them to match whatever chiffon she was destined to wear. Oh, and furs, stoles, capes, coats—everyone had furs.

"My parents were here every time there was a function. I grew weary of it. It's an easy place to come for a good meal, but other than that, I don't do my part. After all these years, I have no regrets about that. It's always been run by men for men, a closed society to maintain something they call history. I think they rewrite it a little to shine the best light on themselves, though we all do that, I suppose."

Jude heard a bitterness in Birdie's tone, something she wasn't articulating. She watched Birdie's face as she glanced at other patrons, watched her tilt her head when people gave her a wave. It piqued Jude's curiosity about Birdie's history. She wondered what Birdie was hinting at when she refused to be the debutant her parents wanted.

Birdie had indicated she'd never married. Jude thought Birdie was an attractive woman, fit, and fashionably dressed. Her hair wasn't colored, but it was an attractive style with pleasing streaks of gray framing her face. It was thick, and she could pull it back from her face and look quite sophisticated.

This evening she had worn a pair of black palazzo pants with a tailored, white silk blouse, the collar turned up around her neck. She wore a large dinner ring on her right hand that glistened when she picked up her martini.

"You should have your portrait painted in that outfit, Birdie," Jude said. "You look very elegant."

Birdie smiled, her eyes crinkling and sparkling in the candlelight from a globe on the table. "Thank you. I'm glad you like my outfit. This is my uniform. I'll have it cleaned next week so I can pack it for my trip. Speaking of that, have you given any thought to what I said about the house-sitting?"

"Well, as a matter of fact, as I was getting ready to come to dinner, I made a decision. It was something Barry said."

"Barry," Birdie bristled. "Did he say something on the phone?"

"No, I read his book, the one up in the guest room. It made me feel a little guilty that I haven't been the survivor I should've been."

"Oh, for heaven's sake. He really hasn't either."

"Why can't you give him some credit, Birdie? His writing is heartfelt, and he's had so many losses."

"Yes, he has had losses, and I was right there with him. My parents, his parents, we all were devastated by the loss of his siblings. The community rallied and supported our family. It was so wonderful to feel that love. The death of my parents, my brother and his wife, were met with the same support. I was stunned that we could have such loss and be surrounded with that kind of kindness. However, I experienced a loss that was so isolating, so unbelievably sad, so maddening, it made me wonder if all that support and kindness was genuine." Birdie stared at the candle under the globe on the table. She seemed to have entered her own thoughts. Jude wondered if she should say anything.

"Let's just say everyone has losses. You don't have to write a book about them to get on with your life. You should be proud of how far you have come, young lady. Your losses started much earlier than Barry's. I don't want to talk about this. Just tell me if I can count on you for some house-sitting?"

"Sure, I can do it. That's the decision I reached. I think I can find a job online also, so I can start working. I'll pace this finding myself task. I have to get used to not having Casey as my guide."

"You can guide yourself, for heaven's sake," Birdie huffed. "It's perfect that you'll be able to stick around. Let's celebrate." Birdie held her empty martini glass up and looked toward the waiter.

CHAPTER 15

BIRDIE

EFRAM BROUGHT THEM fresh drinks followed by a salad. Birdie's favorite part of the meal was the salad; it was always fresh, with just the right amount of dressing. She stole glances of Jude enjoying bites. They shared a hot roll, and then Jude sat back with her wine and said it was the best salad she had ever eaten.

"It's always good. I'm glad you enjoyed it. I was just thinking that you need closure with Casey. She was your friend, and there has been no ceremony to complete that friendship and give you some peace about her passing.

"I would like to propose a toast to your friend Casey. May her spirit continue to soar and find new adventures, and may you be reunited with her and recognize her so you can show her your own soaring spirit."

"Cheers to Casey," Jude said. "That's a nice tribute. However, your candle ceremony during the storm also touched me. You are quite the improviser, Ms. Birdie, when it comes to ritual observances."

Birdie considered Casey probably deserved a more fitting accolade, but she wasn't much for getting too sentimental about someone she had never met. She looked away from Jude and watched the light dance on the surface of the pool. She had thought before Jude arrived that she had life figured out. She was living a routine existence, needing very little and comfortable with what she had. However, she decided she didn't know a thing. She'd been sheltered, never leaving the place she grew up in except for her college years, and they had been interrupted. She returned to the place she knew, to the familiar and the people she knew. *Who am I to suggest I know anything about life? All I know is it's irritating, and then you die.*

As Dennis helped the waiter deliver the main course, Birdie became pensive and quiet. She thought Jude was right. She didn't give Barry credit for coping with the losses he had suffered. She didn't want to admit that he had reason to be protective and concerned for her. Most people knew her as a tough, no-nonsense woman, but she had been broken, and that break had healed into a raised knot, a scar she had no intention of allowing anyone to touch.

Barry had moved on to something different. He'd followed his passion, moving to Houston so he could pursue a legal career in the petroleum industry. He made the contacts he needed and networked, traveling all over the world. That would've frightened Birdie, leaving home, meeting people who didn't know her father and mother, not knowing who to call if she needed something. But Barry figured it out. She had to be proud of that.

Birdie acknowledged that she was afraid. Maybe she wasn't enough. Maybe the real world, off the island, wouldn't approve of her. She could shun the local expectations, but she might not be able to compete with the outside world.

They ate quietly, and when the waiter arrived to take the plates, Birdie had finished two martinis. Her face felt warm and she hesitated to talk. Dennis approached the table to ask if they enjoyed the meal and if they wanted dessert.

"I found a mermaid on the beach, Dennis," Birdie said.

"Well, good for you, Ms. Barnes. Did you leave her there, or did you put her in your bathtub?"

"This is her, Dennis, my friend Jude."

Dennis raised his brows at Jude and smiled. "I had no idea mermaids could walk."

"They do, Dennis. They walk and talk. I would appreciate a cup of decaffeinated coffee, please. How about you, Jude?"

"I'll have regular, please. I don't care for dessert. Thank you." As soon as Dennis walked off, Jude turned to Birdie. "Is that how you talk when you've had two martinis, Birdie, or are you having visions of mermaids?"

"I just like to give people something to talk about. You sound like Barry. I can have a little fun if I want to, give them a reason to cluck their tongues about Birdie Barnes."

Jude sighed and stared at Birdie. "Is there anything I should know about you, Birdie? Do you have bodies buried under your house or something?"

Birdie slapped her leg and laughed out loud. "Wouldn't that be something? My life's been an open book. At least I thought so until you arrived. Now I'm wondering if I've been living it to the fullest. I'll figure it out. Just like you, I have some work to do. This little trip I have coming up should help me put things into perspective, get away for a while, think about things. I'm happy I can count on you to look after Ollie and the house. That's a weight off my mind."

"Happy to help, Birdie. This has been a wonderful meal in a delightful setting. I'd appreciate it if you would allow me to drive us home."

123

"I won't fight you on that. I'll allow it. I need to see if you can drive anyway. You'll be using my car while I'm gone, and I need to know it's in good hands." Birdie reached in her purse and handed Jude the keys.

Dennis opened the patio door for them, and Birdie ushered Jude over to a table full of people and made introductions. She did not falter, nor shoot them the finger.

"You see, Jude, I can do it when I want to," Birdie said as they walked to the car. "It's the desire that alludes me, the willingness to put on the face and betray my feelings. You say I'm good at improvising a formality, and I suppose I am. I guess I've been improvising my whole life."

CHAPTER 16

JUDE

JUDE WAS HAVING second thoughts about her agreement to do the house-sitting. Their ride back from the Club was uneventful, though Birdie's mood seemed altered. She was confrontational at the Club, slightly aloof and cryptic with the other diners. It was a side of Birdie that Jude hadn't observed. She was a little surly with the staff, something that made Jude feel uncomfortable.

As Jude undressed for bed, putting her jewelry on the dresser, she thought about how nice Birdie looked for their outing. She had obviously taken care to make herself more than presentable, but her demeanor didn't match her elegant appearance. Jude had trouble identifying what the problem might be. There wasn't a precursor to Birdie's behavior.

Jude selected a book from the shelf by a female author, Sandra Brown. She planned to read after she brushed her teeth and washed her face, but her thoughts continued to focus on Birdie's mood. She wondered if she hadn't been around that many middle-aged women. Jude had missed having a consistent mother figure due to her moves in foster care. She always wondered if there was something wrong with her. However, after a stint in counseling when she was eighteen, Jude came to the conclusion that all three of her foster mothers were dealing with their own flawed histories and feelings of inadequacy. Her counselor pointed out to her that their behaviors were not always focused on caretaking, and many times they simply enjoyed the attention they received for opening their homes to children not their own.

The therapist explained to Jude that it was common in the helping professions and in fostering families to find people who were simply meeting their own needs, and addressing the needs of the children was sometimes secondary. Of the families Jude had resided in, she only had one father figure who she felt close to. The other parents were more focused on their appearance at church or other organizations in their communities. When they were in the home, the foster children were left to their rooms, or isolated in other ways. Jude knew that probably wasn't true of all foster families, but it had been her experience.

Jude looked at herself in the mirror after she had washed her face. *I was probably very difficult to love. After all, I was the common denominator in all those situations.* She wasn't open to others, even from a young age. She was guarded and awkward about social contacts. She remembered one of her favorite teachers always smiling at her and telling her positive things, and she somehow knew that Mrs. Ramirez understood. Sometimes Jude wished she could go home with her. It would've been much better if she could've lived with Mrs. Ramirez.

Once Jude leaned over the pew in church and asked the family in front of her if they thought she could live with them. They had two small children, and Jude thought maybe she could babysit and do chores. The woman got tears in her eyes and shook her head as she glanced at her husband. Jude sat back against the pew, knowing she had done the wrong thing.

Now here she was again, staying in a house not her own, trying to fit in, trying to figure things out. Maybe she was thinking too hard. She recognized Birdie's house was the nicest one she had ever slept in. It was comfortable and elegant without being stuffy. She hadn't looked around in the other bedrooms upstairs, but the one she occupied was elegant by her standards.

Jude found Birdie to be a clean and uncluttered type of person. She wore simple clothing, sparse jewelry, and very little makeup. Her graying hair was medium length and was appealing both down or twisted up on the back of her head in a clip. She seemed to prefer tunic tops with pockets. Jude noticed that she was always putting something in or taking something out of her pockets. She had three pairs of reading glasses she kept in various places in the house: next to her chair, by the mail in the kitchen, and there were almost always glasses pushed to the top of her head.

She was making a commitment to live with this woman for a while. Jude wondered if she should've waited to agree to such a thing. However, Birdie had been kind to take her in and make sure she got her belongings back. She provided shelter during the storm and made sure Jude had clean clothes and something to eat. She was probably letting her imagination run away with her, even considering that Birdie might not be stable.

Do I even know anyone who is stable?

Jude smiled to herself as she crawled into bed, thinking she might not be able to recognize normal. Everyone had a story of some kind. She imagined Velma and Wendell staring at her from under their umbrella the day after the storm. They certainly didn't look normal, but they could be the poster children for it. What did she know?

One of my problems is that I question everything. Jude decided she had too much time to think. She needed to take on some work projects to keep her occupied. Her degree was in marketing and graphic design, and she intended to check on internet design jobs she could do online. That would give her some income and something to do. Maybe Birdie had some projects around the house she could do. She would make it a point to ask. She needed a purpose. If Jude was going to be living in Birdie's house for more than a month, she needed to decide how she would be spending her days. She didn't think she wanted Birdie to feel responsible for planning them. She also didn't want to interfere with Birdie's normal routine.

Jude sat on the side of the bed, her bare feet dangling. She took a deep breath, aware the effects of the wine were still with her but not so much as to muddle her thoughts. Jude was thinking more clearly than she had in days. She needed to plan for how she would make a living and how she would fill her time. The control over those decisions was hers.

She had plugged her laptop in to charge. Tomorrow she would spend the day researching jobs. Other concerns— Birdie's quirks, her own health, plans for after the house-sitting—those could wait.

CHAPTER 17

BIRDIE

THE CLOSET HAD the cedar odor Birdie enjoyed. She hadn't
thought about it in a long time, but as she was undressing, she
recognized the spicy aroma. She hung her clothing as she
reprimanded herself for allowing old wounds to surface at the
Club. She wanted to have a pleasant dinner with Jude, and she
regretted that she might have acted curt with Dennis. She knew
her behavior was less than pleasant.

Birdie didn't like that rebellious part of her—that part that
wouldn't let the past go. There was an irreverence in the
behavior she never liked about herself, but it belonged to her
and always had. It got her in trouble. No one had ever accused
Birdie of being a conformist.

After she slipped into her gown, Birdie went to the
bathroom. She smoothed lotion onto her lower arms, looking at

the veins and spots covering the backs of her hands. It had been many years since she had the smooth, flawless skin of her youth. *The skin might have been smooth, but the times were tough.* It did seem that something was always lacking. *Okay, snap out of it. What can you be grateful for?* She reminded herself of the mantra Henry always recommended when she was feeling frustrated or sad. It struck Birdie as odd that she seldom reminded herself of her mother's words; it was always Henry's.

Birdie knew immediately the answer to her question. She was grateful that she had found Jude on the beach. Jude was a reminder of her youth, someone who could help her with Ollie while she was away on a trip, but also a reason to alter her routine, a challenge. Maybe Birdie had been in denial all these many years, blaming others for her angry feelings when they were only hers all along. Those who knew her best would say she was having one of her spells, but they didn't really know. They couldn't know because she didn't tell them. That would be the hardest thing, an admission.

She recalled talking with Jude about Barry's loss. She had that very conversation once with her friend Maxine. They sat in Maxine's bedroom after a particularly nasty meltdown in the living room at one of her friend's many cocktail parties. Maxine liked an occasion to use her remarkable crystal cocktail shaker.

"You think you're the only one who's suffered a loss that didn't provoke support from the community, Birdie?" Maxine blared at her. "Get a grip. You have no idea what other people deal with while you're wallowing in your own pity. You ever thought about what it's like to have a miscarriage and not be able to mention it to anyone because your husband didn't want to tell anyone you were pregnant? Huh, Birdie? And think about it, why would a man not want anyone to know his wife was pregnant? Could it be he had another woman watching everything he did? Stuff it, Birdie. Just stuff it."

Birdie replayed Maxine's lecture over and over in her head. She never even asked Maxine for specifics. She could only wipe her tears and tell herself her friend was right, that she had no idea what others had been through. She sat on the side of Maxine's bed, not wanting to walk through the living room to the front door. She would sit there until the other guests left, halting gasps of her sobs escaping her as her eyes wanted to close against the painful lamp light. She wanted to curl up on Maxine's bed and fall asleep under Mildred Odell's mink coat. It could've been lovely there. She didn't do it though. Birdie was afraid she would fall asleep and all those retrieving their coats would gawk.

Opening the medicine cabinet, Birdie looked at the labels on the bottles, moving the pills she had taken by mistake to a higher shelf. She didn't want to make that mistake again. It bothered her that Barry had found out. He might think she wasn't lucid, capable of making silly mistakes like taking medicine from a bottle she couldn't see. She swallowed an aspirin.

Ollie watched her from his pillow. Birdie wondered what he was thinking about the past few days. They had strayed from their daily routine. *It must be confusing for him.* He watched her, and she imagined he was telling her that he really didn't care about the routine as long as his food and water were kept handy. *It's me who relies on routine, and I do it so I don't have to face anything out of the ordinary.*

Birdie wondered if she would be as complicated if she were a dog. *Anyone who observes me probably thinks I'm as simple and predictable as can be, but that's just not true.*

The coming weekend might be one that Barry would come for his routine visit. She hoped he would put it off. She didn't feel like attending church and hosting him while Jude was there. Although, he might be relieved that someone would be there to keep an eye on the house while she was traveling. She hung her robe on the hook on the bathroom door, telling herself not to worry about something that might not occur. That was the source of most of her worries, anticipating things that would never happen.

Birdie crawled beneath the covers, thankful to be in bed. She reached for the lamp and turned the switch. At first the room was dark, but she allowed her eyes to adjust and see the faint light filtering in through the drawn lace curtains. She could imagine the cool lining of Mildred's mink coat touching her skin. She always thought about crawling under that fur. It would've been a comfortable place.

Birdie listened to Ollie's breathing, already a slight snore. She wished she could fall into sleep so readily. Birdie would remember all the times she had been rude and restless, reliving the situations and feelings that weighed on her. She would rehash the times when she could no longer stay in a room while her parents talked about their plans for her. No one asked her what she thought, and no one could see who she was. They only saw who they wanted her to be. She played those stories over in her mind, unable to maintain the vision of curling up on Maxine's bed next to the fragrant lining of Mildred Odell's coat. If Mildred only knew the pleasure the fantasy of that coat brought Birdie. Her husband, Otis, would've been delighted that they got their money's worth.

The full-length mirror that stood in the corner of her bedroom as a girl was now downstairs in the master bedroom. Birdie could see the light shimmering on the reflective surface. It seemed like yesterday that she stood in front of it, practicing the debutant bow she would be required to execute at the balls from November through Mardi Gras. There would be gowns, teas, parades, and grand parties. The things her parents had dreamed about since she was born. It was her legacy to be *presented*.

Birdie's mother kept pressing her about going shopping for the clothing she would need for the "season," as she called it. Birdie kept putting her off, saying she didn't have time. Finally, she got in touch with her mother's best friend, Doris Lazor. There was no one her mother spent more time with. She met with Mrs. Lazor at their appliance store on Broadway. They sat in a back room while Mr. Lazor waited on customers, glancing at them suspiciously.

"I'm going to college," Birdie told Mrs. Lazor. "I don't have time to participate in this nonsense. It's making me feel like I might break their hearts if I tell them." Birdie's eyes filled with tears, but they weren't for her parents. She suspected Mrs. Lazor thought they might be.

"I'll call your mother, Birdie. Don't fret over this. It's not the end of the world if you don't want to participate." Mrs. Lazor gave a forced laugh. I'd imagine your father might be relieved and thankful he can save a little money, don't you think?" Mrs. Lazor patted her arm. Birdie knew she really didn't understand. She and her husband had four boys. Her dreams never involved shopping for the requisite white gown or the many other accessories required for coming out. Birdie didn't know who else to trust with the confidence.

Mrs. Lazor did telephone Birdie's mother. When Birdie got home that day, she went straight to her room and didn't respond to her mother's calls from the bottom of the stairs. She threw herself across her bed and closed her eyes, imagining herself as a different person, one who could fulfill the dreams of her parents, one meant to be a debutant. She opened her eyes and looked into the full-length mirror. Her long dark hair hung over her shoulder. Her mother's calls ceased. Birdie listened for the footfalls she thought would be coming up the stairs; they didn't come.

Staring herself in the eyes, Birdie remained in front of the mirror. Then she walked to the desk in the corner of the room, opened her sewing basket, and rummaged through the contents. It was Saturday night. Girls her age were preparing to go out to the movies. She was home for the weekend from college, but there were no plans. Birdie was only there to try to get the courage to tell her parents that she didn't want to participate in their social plans for her.

She found what she was looking for and returned to the mirror. Standing in front of it, she couldn't look herself in the eyes again. Birdie gathered her thick hair in her fist and began to jab at it with gnawing swipes of the scissors. She stared at the wooden floor as her thick, dark hair fell into soft mounds, fluttering from her grip.

CHAPTER 18

JUDE

NOT AGAIN, JUDE thought. She entered the kitchen to discover Birdie wasn't there. She was nervous about approaching the bedroom, deciding to make coffee first. Maybe the aroma would entice Birdie out of her room.

When Jude entered the den, Ollie was standing by the back door. She let him out, then went to the front door to go out and get the newspaper. By the time Jude reentered the house, Birdie was standing in the hall.

"Good morning, Jude. I didn't sleep well last night. It took me forever to fall asleep. Funny how sometimes I can get in bed dog tired and just can't shut my mind off."

"Good morning. I started the coffee. It won't be long. I fell right to sleep. I think it was the wine." Jude remembered the evening. They had both enjoyed drinks, but didn't overdo it. She wondered what had kept Birdie's mind occupied.

Jude wished she knew her better. She couldn't imagine what would keep Birdie awake at night. Jude had committed to house sit and told herself that Birdie had the greatest risk in the arrangement—it was her house, her belongings, her dog. If anyone should be guessing at someone's character, it should be Birdie.

"Watch this, Jude." Birdie walked to the middle of the den and adjusted her robe around her. She held both of her arms out to her side, parallel with her shoulders. Her right foot slid forward and she made a wide circle with her leg, reaching out far to the side and then gliding back behind her and around. She lowered her torso, all the while keeping her head up and smiling. When her body was as low to the ground as it could go, Birdie bowed her head, her arms still extended, then looked up, smiling broadly. Her right leg retraced the circle and her body was again erect as she lowered her arms.

Jude applauded. "Is that a new yoga move?" she asked.

Birdie laughed. "No, that's the Texas Dip. I practiced that for months. I'll never forget it."

"Well, it looks like you might have practiced it recently. That was pretty smooth."

Birdie sighed. "I don't know why I've been thinking about that, but I have. It kept me awake. I'm a little surprised I could get up. My knees aren't what they used to be."

Jude followed Birdie into the kitchen and watched her pour two mugs of coffee. She reached into the pantry for the cinnamon rolls. "You want yours heated?" Birdie asked.

"No, I'm fine with it room temperature."

"Let's sit on the back porch." Birdie led the way through the French doors and settled into a cushioned wicker chair with the newspaper. Jude set her mug on the coffee table and replenished Ollie's bowls with water and food.

"You're a quick study," Birdie commented. "I appreciate you taking the initiative to feed Ollie. I was inclined to make him wait until I read the news. You better watch out, you're going to be his favorite if you keep that up."

"I'm practicing." Jude sat in the chair across from Birdie. "I know it's not pleasant, but what about Ollie's veterinarian? Do you have all that information written down somewhere? I hope we don't need it while you're gone, but I think I should know."

"You're right. I do have a folder with all his information. I'll get all that together before it's time to go. I can drive you by their offices. We do need to think about those kinds of things and put them in a place that's handy. Good thinking."

Jude didn't know how old Ollie was. She watched him finish his food and walk inside to his pillow. He wasn't a puppy, not playful or very active, but she thought that could be from Birdie's routine.

"How old is Ollie, Birdie?"

Birdie pushed her glasses to the top of her head and folded the newspaper onto her lap. "Let's see. I adopted him when he was two from the shelter, and I've had him for at least ten years. Velma's son was still alive. I remember him walking down here to visit that first year I had Ollie. Gino, we called him, clever boy. He had Down syndrome, but he would sneak out of the house when Velma took a nap and come knock on my door in the afternoon. Ollie and I liked to see him coming. That little dog didn't take to many people, but he would curl up in Gino's lap and let him stroke his ears. I always thought Ollie knew Gino wasn't long for this world."

"What happened to him?" Jude asked.

"He'd always had problems, spells with his breathing or something. Velma was always rushing him to the hospital. I think he was thirty-two when he died. Velma and Wendell haven't been the same since.

Gino got the biggest kick out of Barry. Of course, Barry was much younger, but Gino was all smiles if Barry was around. Barry spoke at his funeral. I hadn't thought about that in a long time. It hadn't been that long since we lost my brother and sister-in-law."

"That was in his book," Jude recalled. "I remember a mention of Barry speaking at the funeral of a friend."

"Yes, that was Gino, precious soul."

Jude watched Birdie pull her glasses down from her head and wipe the corners of her eyes before resuming with the paper. The answer to her question was Ollie wasn't a young dog. He was getting up in age.

Birdie was moving through emotions in the last couple of days. Jude had experienced a shift with her. Her first impressions were a kind, mellow woman, a little crusty with her neighbors, but basically relaxed and easygoing. Now she was discovering layers, brewing remembrances, a collection of experiences she could call to the forefront and muster an intense feeling.

There had been no older women in Jude's life, no grandmother or aging aunts. The women all belonged to someone else. Their laps weren't available for a crushed spirit. There were no kind words for disappointments. A few teachers seemed approachable, but Jude never chanced it. What if they turned her away or told her she was silly for her feelings?

She watched Birdie as if she might be an alien visiting the planet. Jude wanted information about what to expect, but she sensed Birdie wasn't sure what to expect. Each revisit to a memory triggered a reaction that seemed to surprise even Birdie.

"I'm going to get another cup of coffee," Birdie said, folding the paper and setting it aside. "How about you?"

"Yes, I'll have another." Jude followed Birdie to the kitchen.

"How blunt can I be with you, Birdie?" Jude said. "I mean, we've only known each other a few days. Are we friends? Are you my employer? What are we?"

"We are friends because I trust you," Birdie said after looking into Jude's eyes. "I haven't given it much thought, but maybe it's your age. I think of you like I think of Barry—a member of my family, someone who I'd do anything for, but maybe they irritate me occasionally."

"Am I irritating you?"

"No, not now, but I can see you might have the potential," Birdie giggled.

"This is weird, huh?" Jude said.

"It could be. I suppose other people would think so, but I've lived long enough to see weird. There are many stranger things than finding someone on the beach at just the right time of your life. You might be thinking it was fortuitous for you, but I can be a little selfish and think you came to me at the right time."

"I see what you mean. It can work out for both of us, can't it? As long as I'm not a burden and I can do something to earn my keep." Jude walked back toward her seat on the porch. Birdie turned off the coffee pot and followed her.

"I was just thinking a while ago that I've never had a woman in my life, an older woman, like a grandmother or an aunt. There were those women, but they were never mine. They belonged to my foster siblings. I only watched them from a distance. I never asked for their hugs or approached them because I was afraid they would … maybe they would shoo me away or something.

"I watch you remembering and see your emotions. I've never experienced that. I don't know if you're normal?"

"Well, guess what? I don't know if I'm normal either." Birdie laughed. "How does anyone know if they're normal, Jude? I haven't figured that out after all these years, so surely you don't expect to hold the answers.

"Here's what I know. Everyone has a story, and everyone reacts in a different way to the same circumstance. That's all I know. I can only be responsible for myself, and the mistakes I've made in that regard could fill the Gulf of Mexico. I try to do no harm, but sometimes I fail and when I do, it's never intentional. I'm just a woman getting older and still searching for the meaning of my life."

Jude had never talked so openly with another person. She had been to counseling with foster parents, but she had never said what she felt. She only said what she thought others wanted to hear. She thought that might've been because she didn't trust. She trusted Birdie, and Birdie seemed to trust her, so she decided to be honest. If Birdie asked her questions, she would tell the truth. She just hadn't asked the right questions yet.

There were so many questions Birdie could ask, questions that would force Jude to expose herself. Since the accident, there were new concerns, burdens Jude didn't want to share. Birdie was right, everyone filtered their experiences through their own history. Whatever shapes a person may never be known by anyone else.

CHAPTER 19

BIRDIE

IT WAS NICE to see that Jude felt comfortable with Ollie and wanted to get into a routine. They went for a walk, the morning walk on the beach. Jude pulled ahead and gathered seashells in her pockets. She had taken off her shoes and carried them under her arm so she could wade into the water and wash the sand from the shells.

Birdie followed at a distance, noticing Jude. She remembered doing the same things when she was younger, coming to the beach to escape the house. She usually walked out in a huff after an argument with her mother, running until she got to Avenue M, where she would duck down the alley so she could hide in the oleanders if anyone came looking for her. The biggest fights were over her choice in clothing or the way she wanted to wear her hair. However, the ultimate was much later, when she was in college. The season.

"Bullshit," Birdie would scream at her mother. "It's all bullshit. You're willing to spend thousands of dollars to present me for what? Save your money, mama. It's 1968. People don't arrange marriages anymore." She always slammed the door for dramatic effect.

Sometimes Birdie would call Henry before she left the house and he would meet her on the beach. They would sit below the seawall on the granite boulders so her father wouldn't see them if he drove around looking for her. Henry carried his bicycle on his shoulder down the steep steps. Sometimes they would smoke marijuana, but most of the time they just shared a beer. A passerby would stare; they were an odd couple in the late sixties.

"If they make me go through with this, Henry, I'll need a date, someone to escort me. Do you think you can do that? Escort me?" Birdie sat cross-legged on the edge of one of the big granite boulders.

"Hell no, Birdie. No way. First of all, you know my mother doesn't have the money for all that. Second of all, I'm black. You ever seen a black guy at those deals? Number three, I love

147

you, but not enough for all the drama that would cause. There's probably a bunch of other reasons, but I think number two disqualifies me pretty good." Henry stood next to his bicycle, propped against a large piece of driftwood. He stared up at Birdie, his forehead puckered in parallel lines above his eyes, but then he smiled. All Birdie could see were his white teeth.

"I won't do it, then. If you can't be there with me, I can't do it. All those people staring at you, waiting for you to fall down or something. It's just not me, Henry. It's Camille, but it's not me."

"Yes, it is Camille. Maybe she could talk to your mother for you. She could explain it in a way that wouldn't mention the real reason." Henry climbed up the granite rock to sit next to Birdie.

"What do you mean?"

"You know what I'm talking about, Birdie. When are you going to get real with yourself? That's your whole problem right there. It's not your mama and daddy. It's you. They're left in the dark trying to figure you out. They think they're giving you what every girl would want, and you're fighting them like a pole cat in a brown paper bag."

"You're full of shit, Henry. You always have been. That's why your eyes are brown. You're so full of shit that your boogers look like chocolate chips."

"Oh yeah, well, your mama's so fat she sat on the sofa and when she stood up, the cushion was wedged between her crack."

Birdie started laughing so hard she blew beer out her nose. Then Henry laughed. "At least when I blow boogers out of my nose they don't look like beer foam."

He had a way of removing Birdie from the turmoil in her head. With Henry, everything could be calm and easy. There was no reason to pretend. He was Birdie's only soft place to fall. He knew her soul and her deepest desires. He had given her an idea about telling her mother through a friend that she wouldn't participate as a debutant. Since third grade, Henry had been Birdie's best friend, but no one even knew that except Henry's cousin Eldon.

Birdie would like nothing better than to walk in the front door with Henry at her side and tell her mother that he was staying for dinner. She wanted her parents to love him as much as she did. That wasn't going to happen because Henry was a genuine person and he couldn't hide anything. Her parents were about making a good impression.

"I have something to tell you, Birdie. Now just hear me out. You know they're going to start drafting people for the war. They're calling up more troops, so I decided I might as well enlist."

Birdie gasped. "You can't do it, Henry. There's a chance you'll have a high number. You won't have to go. It's not something we should be doing anyway, dropping all those bombs on those innocent people in Vietnam. How can you think that's okay, Henry? That's not you. You can't possibly think that's what you want to do."

"Look, Birdie, where else can I get an opportunity to travel, get some benefits for going to school later? You know there's no chance my mama can pay for college classes. I need to get out of this town. You're not here anymore anyway. You're off at college. Eldon and I are going to join up together."

"No, not Eldon! Henry, please don't do this. Do you know what war does to people? You'll come back different, angry, or not at all. Please, please don't go, Henry. Don't leave me here alone. I'm not that far away. I can be home when I don't have classes. Please don't go."

"You won't be alone. You have your parents and your brother. Get yourself together, Birdie. It's going to be okay. It's an opportunity for me."

"Opportunity! Shit, Henry, you've been talking to some jive recruiter who's blown smoke up your ass. War is not an opportunity. We shouldn't even be in this war. You know that. We've talked about it a hundred times." Birdie looked away from him. She had tears in her eyes, and she could feel a blubbering cry coming from her chest. She hid her face, holding her hand to her mouth.

"Look, I don't have the same opportunity you have here, Birdie. You're worried about some social season bullshit, and I have to decide whether I'll enlist or get caught up in the civil rights protests here. Mama is encouraging me to go to Vietnam. She thinks it's the most patriotic thing to do. Either way, Mama thinks my days are numbered. I can get killed in a protest by cops, or I can go travel and get killed by the Viet Cong."

"Patriotic?" Birdie was calmer, listening to Henry's reasoning. It made no sense to her, but she knew his experience in the world was totally different from hers. They shared the same philosophy, but not the same experience. "You know, I never expected you to wrap yourself in a flag and carry a gun."

"I know. It's not an easy decision. I was hoping you could tell me it would be okay."

Birdie stared out at the water, tears glistening in her eyes. She picked up Henry's hand, sandwiching it between both of hers. "You'll come back. You and Eldon will come back, and we'll have a barbecue to welcome you home. I promise to write to you. I will. I'll write to Eldon, too. I think I can be okay, Henry. It makes my dilemma pretty stupid."

Henry put his arm around Birdie and held her while she sobbed. He cried, too, for both of them. Birdie was caught in a different kind of trap, and he knew it bound her just as tight as the color of his skin.

"We're quite a pair," Birdie said, wiping the tears from her cheeks. "An impossible pair."

"Well, I know you are, but what am I?" Henry joked.

"It's not funny, Henry."

Birdie allowed Ollie to run to Jude as she approached them on the beach. He didn't prance the way he used to, but he still had some spunk.

Jude held her hand open to show Birdie she had found a sand dollar and some sea glass. They walked back to the public shower so Jude could rinse her feet and put on her shoes. Birdie was sullen. Her thoughts of Henry made her remember their times on the beach. Seeing Eldon when he brought Jude's backpack hit Birdie in a way she didn't expect. They were aging. Too much time had gone by, and she didn't even realize it was happening. She was afraid Henry would be disappointed. His life ended and hers was frozen in time, not moving from place or position, just there.

CHAPTER 20

JUDE

BIRDIE TOOK A container down from the shelf in her closet to show Jude the sea glass she had collected. There were photos, letters, and collected treasures. She held up a bundle of letters. Jude didn't know what they were, but Birdie wiped a tear from her eye.

Jude sat at the kitchen table eating a turkey sandwich, watching Birdie pick through the contents of her treasure box.

"Look at this old photo. That's Velma, and that little boy beside her is Gino."

"Oh my." Jude wiped mayonnaise from her lips. "She was beautiful."

Birdie smiled, glancing at the photo again. "We were young. Enjoy your youth, Jude. It can get away from you, and before you know it you're looking at pictures of yourself, wondering where that girl went."

Jude felt Birdie slipping into one of her sullen moods. "You know, I can make some jewelry from that sea glass," Jude said. "I took a class once. It sits in a box and no one ever gets to admire it. You could wear those pieces with that lovely outfit you wore the other night."

"Wouldn't that be nice?" Birdie held the pieces of glass in her palm, rolling them around with her fingers. "Well, take these pieces and surprise me." Birdie handed Jude the glass. "I'm supposed to go shopping with the girls tomorrow in Houston. The more I think about that, the more I dread the whole thing. Maybe I'll just call and beg off. I have enough clothing for the cruise. I don't need to waste my time or money." Birdie sighed. Jude could feel the air in the room become heavy with Birdie's apathy.

Jude took another bite of sandwich and a sip of tea. "Birdie, you're so much like me. When I think about it, it's like listening to myself. I'm an introvert. I know I am. That's what Casey always said. I find reasons why I don't want to be with people. I never thought I was good enough because of the foster care moves." Jude pursed her lips, trying to think how she could explain herself to Birdie.

"When Casey would insist I go out with her, I would always have a great time when I got there, but I dreaded it before I went. I think if you go out with your friends, you'll see it's just what you need. Once you're with them, you'll enjoy their company."

Birdie busied herself putting things back in her box. She pushed her half-eaten sandwich away. "So, you think I'm an introvert?"

"No, Birdie, I think I'm an introvert, and you remind me of myself when you talk that way."

"I should make myself go on this shopping trip, even though this minute, it's the last thing I want to do?"

"Yes, you should talk yourself into it. Let's think about what you might add to your wardrobe. It would be nice to buy something new. Hey, let's go to one of those walk-in nail places and get pedicures. If you're on a cruise, you're going to want your feet to look nice in your sandals."

Birdie smiled. "I suppose you're right. I had been looking forward to this trip. It's perfect that you're here to take care of things. Mama would tell me to get happy in the same pants I got mad in."

"Are you mad?" Jude asked. She looked at Birdie with wide eyes.

"No, not really. I'm restless, like I've missed something, but I don't know what it is." Birdie rubbed her forehead, then stood and picked up the plates from the table.

Jude stood also, grabbing the glasses. She walked to the sink behind Birdie. "If you don't go shopping and miss the cruise, you *will* miss something. You'll miss being with your friends and playing that game you like on the ship."

"Maybe I could find one of those long caftan deals people wear over their swimsuits, and a straw hat."

"Yes, you should get orange or red, and get a new lipstick to go with it." Jude filled the sink with sudsy water. "Let's go to the drugstore and get some lipstick and nail polish to match. Then we can get pedicures. You can wear the lipstick shopping tomorrow and pick out the perfect caftan."

Birdie dried her hands and threw the towel on the counter. "I'm going to comb my hair and get my purse."

Jude washed the dishes. She was often reframing Birdie's negative thoughts and regrets to mollify her. She recalled Casey doing the same thing with her.

Ollie sat at Jude's feet, staring up at her. It was his standard request for a dog treat. Jude walked to the treat jar, then asked Ollie to sit before delivering the biscuit. "Everyone needs stroking today," she whispered. She had a selfish thought that it would be nice to have the house to herself while Birdie was away shopping. She hoped Birdie didn't change her mind again.

Jude made a list of the things she would need from the craft section of the discount store to make Birdie jewelry from the sea glass. They could probably get the lipstick and nail polish from the pharmacy at the same store.

Her laptop was still plugged into the charger on Birdie's dining room table. Jude hadn't had time to check the websites she intended to research for job opportunities. She had kept a list of possibilities for her graphic design skills; maybe when they returned from shopping, she would have a chance to do some searching.

"Okay, I'm ready." Birdie appeared in the kitchen, freshened and cheery.

CHAPTER 21

BIRDIE

OUT IN THE afternoon sunshine, Birdie felt more optimistic about the shopping trip. She often thought she couldn't compete with the fashion sense of her friends. They shopped at the ritzy places around River Oaks, and she was more comfortable with the clearance rack in the department stores. However, a new caftan would be reasonable and not take too much room in her suitcase. She could wrap her head around that, and maybe a hat or scarf.

Birdie drove while Jude gazed out the window at the people on the beach. "It's busy today." She said.

"The weekend's always busy in nice weather. You know what they say about these people on the beach? They come from Houston with their bathing suits under their clothing and twenty dollars in their pockets, and they never change either one."

Jude laughed. "Does that mean they don't do much shopping?"

"Yes, I suppose some disgruntled merchant made that joke. However, I see people milling around down on the Strand. They do seem to be spending money on the island."

"But you and your friends go to Houston to shop?"

"Not my choice," Birdie said. "There are a couple of cute stores I like here. They don't want to be seen in the same outfit as someone else. I'm not opposed to it. Imitation is a form of flattery, don't you think?"

"I'd agree with that. So you just go along to get along?"

"I don't want to rock the boat. I watch other people to see how I'm supposed to act." Birdie turned the blinker on to turn into the parking lot where they would park.

"You know how to act, Birdie. What are you talking about?"

"I'm not like other people. Never have been. I've always been different, not the same as my friends. I'm a weirdo, Jude. Of all the women for you to find on the beach to be a role model, you hook up with Birdie Barnes, the weirdo."

Jude didn't respond to those comments. It was a little like the conversation at the Club, the night of their dinner. Birdie knew she confused people when she spouted off about how weird she was. She didn't care. *Let them see what that feels like for a while. Let them find out what it feels like for people around*

159

you to make no sense. She decided they would get the shopping over quickly and get on with the toe painting.

"You go get your bangle stuff, Jude. I'm going to step right over to the cosmetics. I don't have patience for this place. All these people milling around make me nervous. Meet me at the express checkout when you're done."

Birdie power walked toward the cosmetics while Jude headed to crafts. The lipsticks were overwhelming. She hadn't shopped for one in a while. There were glosses, matte, wand, pencils. "For the love of Pete," she whispered to herself. *I'd have to have instructions for some of this shit.* She settled for a rosy color that bordered on purple, then changed her mind. *That's a color for autumn.* She talked herself out of it because Jude had said orange or red. Jude had some fashion sense; that, she decided, she should listen to. Birdie's eyes gravitated toward the reds. She found a color called "red-orange," then went to the polish. Holding the lip color up to the bottles and tilting her head back to gaze through her glasses, Birdie selected one.

Feeling confident about her choices, she headed toward the main aisle. The end cap caught her eye. There was a display of reading glasses, marked half off. There among them was a pair of round frames in her prescription, the exact color of her new lipstick. She stood in front of the small mirror at the top of the display, her reading glasses pushed to the top of her head while she tried on the red frames. She held the polish bottle and lipstick up to her face, trying to get all the items into her view in the mirror. She glanced down to see a child staring up at her. Birdie pursed her lips, then stuck out her tongue. She thought better of it.

"I'm sorry. I didn't mean to do that. Don't grow up to be mean like me. Now, go find your mother." Birdie walked off with the glasses in her hand.

Jude approved of the colors and thought the glasses were adorable when Birdie modeled them for her.

"There's a nail salon just down this strip center. We don't even have to move the car. What did you get, Jude?"

"It's a surprise." Jude held her hands over her purchase. You'll see when the time comes."

They spent most of the rest of the afternoon getting deluxe pedicures and manicures. The session came with complimentary wine. Birdie could not recall the last time she had her toenails painted. She almost fell asleep in the chair when the technician was massaging her feet. She glanced at Jude from time to time, watching her motionless in the chair with her eyes closed. Birdie imagined it was what mothers and daughters experienced when they had outings together.

Jude had been right about the color. Birdie had asked that her new purchase be applied to her nails and toes. It was vivid, perfect for a cruise.

Birdie snapped a picture of Jude in the vibrating chair with a glass of champagne. She put her glasses on to show the technician how wonderful she would look while she sat in a lounge chair reading a book on the deck of the ship.

Birdie listened to the technicians giggle and chatter in Vietnamese as she modeled for them. She wondered what they were saying, suspecting they might be calling her a foolish old woman. That's what she always thought, that people were making fun of her, or saying something negative. Maybe they were saying she looked cute and fun, but she had her doubts.

Jude smiled at her.

Sometimes Birdie didn't know who she was either. Most of the time she didn't think about it at all, but when there were other people around, she wanted them to think she was okay. Later she asked Jude about it. The feeling had been present with her most of the day.

"Of course you're okay, Birdie. You're more than okay. What are you talking about?"

"Do you think those girls in the salon thought the glasses and nail color were okay?"

"You made them giggle. Their eyes were twinkling. The colors were striking, and your face was so full of life and joy. There was a positive energy there, Birdie. I could feel it. But you doubt. That doubt is in your head, not in the faces I was looking at in the salon."

Birdie didn't pursue the conversation. Jude was right. The doubt was in her head, and she carried it around with her. It plagued her sometimes, pulsing in her temples and cautioning her about trying to be normal. Who did she think she was, trying to pass for normal? That's why she was tentative about the shopping trip. Why'd they even invite her to go along? They knew she didn't normally shop in those boutiques.

Maybe she would have a headache in the morning.

CHAPTER 22

JUDE

AFTER RETURNING FROM the afternoon walk to the beach, Jude asked Birdie if she had thought about packing for the cruise. "It's a week away. We're not leaving until next Sunday."

"Yes, but suppose you don't have enough underwear, or you need some toothpaste? Don't you think you should start thinking about those things so you can make a list of what you might need?"

"Oh heavens, you're right. It's such a chore. I thought this was going to be fun."

"I'll help you, Birdie. Let's look at what you need to take."

They spent the rest of the afternoon going through Birdie's closet and selecting versatile items she could mix and match. Birdie opened the suitcase on the sofa in her room. Jude folded the items and layered them with tissue paper, checking off a list.

Jude showed Birdie how to tie a scarf several ways and how to use it as a shawl for cool evenings. She suggested Birdie wear it with her black pants and white silk blouse. They practiced several times tying it so Birdie could wear it as a vest.

"You need another scarf, Birdie, something that's bright, maybe greens and blues or purple. You can wear it as a sarong over your swimsuit, or you can use it with that black jersey top and the cream slacks in the evening. When you're shopping tomorrow, be on the lookout. So, the caftan, a scarf in blues, and a straw hat."

"I can remember that."

The phone rang and Birdie left the room to answer. Jude could hear her talking and assumed it was her friend about the shopping trip. Jude took the cosmetic bag from the pocket of the larger suitcase and put it in the bathroom. When Birdie returned, she was less enthusiastic about packing.

"That was Loretta. We're going to brunch in the morning before we shop. They're picking me up at nine thirty. I suppose I should decide what I'll wear for that. This is just overwhelming. How does a person get through all this?"

Jude laughed. "Wear those navy slacks and that beige sweater with the metallic threads. When you're shopping, get the clerk to help you find a scarf for that outfit, and if they have a chunky necklace that would go with that, it could be another dinner outfit."

"How'd you get so smart?"

"I've always had an eye for color and style. For a while, I was a personal shopper for some ladies in Austin. It was fun. I liked spending other people's money. Most of the people I knew were in retail. I much preferred dealing with customers one at a time." Jude glanced around the room, noticing they had everything organized. "Okay, you have the shoes there. All you need to do is decide on the jewelry you'll take and your cosmetics and you're set. Oh, and your gowns for sleeping. Maybe pack two of those and a robe."

"I don't know what I'd do without you. I'm feeling much better about this now. Would you mind taking Ollie for his walk in the morning? I guess I won't have time if they're coming at nine thirty."

"Of course, no problem." Jude stretched her back and rotated her shoulders. It had been a busy day physically, but she also felt an emotional drain she couldn't put her finger on. It was as if she was on edge, a little worried about Birdie. "I think I'd like some wine, and maybe we could order in a pizza. What do you think?"

"That's a wonderful idea." Birdie clapped her hands. "I'll make the call. I know the best place. The wine is on the counter beside the fridge."

Jude opened the wine and poured two glasses. She could hear Birdie on the phone ordering the pizza, addressing the person on the other end of the line by their first name. She set Birdie's glass on the kitchen table and walked to the back porch with hers. The sky to the west turned orange and then pink through the towering branches of the oak. She could hear a dog barking down the street as a plane flew high overhead. She heard the consistent cadence of the surf a steady metronome of sound.

The clasps and wire Jude bought for the sea glass jewelry were in her purse. She was imagining the items she could make. Her plan was to put them together while Birdie was shopping so she could take them on the cruise.

I'm never going to find time to do the job search.

Birdie appeared with her wine. "Fifteen minutes and we'll have pizza. Excellent idea, Jude. Pizza is my favorite."

"I'm paying, Birdie. When they get here, I'll get the door."

"That's not necessary, Jude. I'm happy to get it."

"I want to. Let me do it, please. I insist. Now, tell me where you'll be going on the cruise."

Birdie explained the ports the cruise would visit and the excursions they had planned. Jude suggested she drop everyone off with their bags.

"Well, that's kind of you. I'll see what the others are doing, but I'm sure that would be great for me. You can just bring the car back here. I hadn't even thought about that. See, that's what I'm talking about, Jude. I'm not good with the details and minutia."

"You'd figure it out, Birdie." Jude thought she could, but she wasn't so sure Birdie would have.

The doorbell rang. Jude grabbed her purse and went to pay for the pizza.

CHAPTER 23

BIRDIE

BIRDIE RODE IN the back seat of Maxine's sedan, a little carsick, and they hadn't even crossed the causeway. Betty and Loretta were talking about their grandchildren. Birdie could see Maxine adjusting her mirror so she could watch her. She groped in her purse for her sunglasses and put them on, not wanting Maxine to see her eyes. It was none of her business what she was looking at.

All of their mothers were dead by now, so Birdie couldn't wonder if her mother was pleading over the phone with theirs to include her in their outings. She always thought they invited her to mah-jongg because they couldn't find a fourth. This group had been the coveted circle in high school, but Birdie had no desire to be a part of their clutch in those days. She preferred her one-on-one conversations with Henry to the gossip and chatter of the girls her mother preferred as her friends.

Their families had always been close, belonging to the same clubs, hosting each other with dinner parties and bridge games, and getting involved in the same civic activities. Birdie was the odd girl, the one not quite fitting in with the others. Her mother always suggested sleepovers and movie outings, but none of those things had appealed to Birdie. Her eyes glazed over when they talked about fashion, or who was dating who. It was such blather. They had no interest in what was happening with the war or the civil rights movement.

Birdie let out deep sighs when they talked about the boys in their class. Their favorite topic was the football players a couple of grades ahead of them. Maxine and Loretta were aspiring cheerleaders. They had often invited Birdie to Saturday afternoon practices in their backyards. Maxine would have her hair wound around large aluminum rollers. Loretta's short Twiggy cut would be taped to her forehead. They needed someone to throw in the air, and Birdie's slight frame made her the perfect candidate. She recalled agreeing to two of these afternoons, but then she told them she would rather paint her fingernails with lighter fluid and set them on fire.

"You're so rude sometimes, Birdie," Maxine complained. "Don't you want to get the practice? Being a cheerleader could really help your social life."

"I'm perfectly happy with my social life. I only need more free time to pursue the things I'm interested in, not what you and Loretta think I should do. Trust me, getting tossed in the air by you two is not my idea of a fun Saturday afternoon."

There were lulls in their outings because of Birdie's blunt responses to what she felt were shallow pursuits. She suspected they only called when her mother complained to their mothers that she was spending too much time by herself going to the beach. The truth was she wasn't by herself. She was with the people who knew her, the ones who accepted her as she was and didn't try to mold her into something she wasn't. Her best friends didn't want to toss her in the air to improve her social life. She couldn't even bring the people she identified with to her house. Birdie feared their rejection, and she feared her own.

Maxine was turning into the parking lot of the restaurant when Birdie had a sinking feeling that it was probably the Sunday Barry would show up to take her to church. She fumbled in her purse for her phone. It wasn't there. She waved her hand in the air, dismissing her forgetfulness. "Shit," she said under her breath.

"What's the matter, Birdie?" Loretta asked. "Did you forget something?"

"My phone."

"Do you need to call someone? You can use mine."

"No, I guess not. She'll figure it out. She's a smart girl, and I'd probably just mess it up."

Birdie decided to let Jude deal with Barry. It was a relief not to have to play the part and accompany him to church that morning. All these women were Catholic, choosing to attend Saturday mass at 5:30 p.m. They had already confessed their sins, accepted the Lord, and were moving on with their plans. Loretta was a convert, choosing to become Catholic when she married. Birdie always suspected Loretta was depending on the no divorce belief, but that hadn't worked out. Like her, they had their weaknesses, but she decided if she had to spend the morning with other people, these were the ones least likely to get on her nerves.

"Tell me about that girl, Birdie," Maxine said. She was tilting her head, looking at Birdie in the rearview mirror. "How do you know her?"

Birdie smiled. She would tell them the truth. Dazzle them with the serendipitous tale of finding a young woman on the beach who could keep her company during the storm, help her plan her wardrobe, and house-sit with Ollie. She would twist her necklace with her freshly polished fingers, purse her lips lined with a luscious red-orange, and amuse them with her luck. But she wouldn't tell them about her recent sullen moods at remembering her own youth. She wouldn't say what she had lost or how she recently realized how much time had escaped her. She couldn't let them know the life she mourned. They wouldn't understand. They had never understood. They had put their gowns on and done the deep bow with honest smiles to sincere cheers of acceptance.

They were intrigued by Jude and wondered at a young woman with no relatives or friends. "How do you get through life and suddenly have no one?" Betty said. "It doesn't seem possible, does it?"

"She has siblings somewhere she might search for," Birdie said. "In the meantime, she has me. I've encouraged her to stay. She's a lovely young woman."

They resumed chatting over eggs benedict and mimosas, excited about the cruise. Birdie dropped her guard, enjoying their company and looking forward to their shopping experience. She wanted them to see her confident, with a goal for the items she needed. She couldn't be one of them, but she knew how to act like one of them. She had done it for a long time.

CHAPTER 24

JUDE

OLLIE WAS FINE with Jude taking him on a morning walk without Birdie. He was obedient. When he was allowed off his leash, he returned and sat to allow Jude to reattach it. She wondered why she hadn't considered getting a dog. Jude remembered pets in some of the foster homes she had lived in. They had attachments to their owners and generally skirted around the children moving in and out.

Jude found more sea glass and intended to work on the jewelry when they were back at the house. She planned to make a pin with earrings, something Birdie might wear on the cruise. She recalled seeing a set in an art gallery on South Congress in Austin. She had examined them closely and looked forward to recreating the look. Jude wanted to make something Birdie would appreciate. She believed she owed her.

The weather was pleasant, with a dry wind coming from the north. Jude had wrapped a light scarf around her neck, pulling it up higher around her ears on the walk back. There were surfers in wet suits sitting on their boards, watching the surf. The change in the wind had flattened the surface of the water and some of them were walking to their cars, carrying their boards above their heads and stripping down to their trunks on the seawall. They were all ages, both male and female. Some of them might've been families. Jude felt a twinge of loss noticing their shared activity.

There were familiar faces among the people Jude saw on the beach and seawall. She suspected they had a routine walk, like Birdie. They, too, expected to see the same faces on their daily trips to the water.

The air was thicker on the island, layered with the salt from the sea and normally heavy with the water that surrounded the area. The constant lapping of the surf against the beach provided a rhythm, a pulse Jude had grown accustomed to. She looked forward to the approaching days of walking Ollie in a predictable routine.

As they crossed the seawall to Birdie's street, Jude thought about the shopping trip. She hoped Birdie wouldn't be disappointed and could find the things she wanted. It had seemed important to her. As they passed the large oleander that blocked the view to Birdie's house, Jude noticed a different car parked on the street in front of the house. It was one that hadn't been there since she arrived, an expensive model, maybe a BMW.

Ollie began to wag his tail and trot faster toward the house, pulling at the leash. Jude quickened her pace to keep up with him. As they mounted the steps, she noticed the front door was open. She could see through the screen, a man in a suit approaching the door from the back of the house. Ollie met him at the door with a feverish wag of his tail.

"Hey, Ollie," he said, then looked toward Jude.

"Hello," she said. "You must be Barry, I hope."

"Yes, I'm Barry, and you're Jude?"

"Yes, yes, I am." Jude held her hand out to shake Barry's extended one. "I wasn't aware you were coming. Birdie didn't say anything. She's off shopping with her friends this morning."

"Shopping? Hmm, that doesn't sound like Birdie. What friends?

"Her mah-jongg group. I'm not sure of their names. I know Maxine picked her up. They went to Houston for brunch and to get things for their cruise."

"Cruise? Birdie didn't tell me they had settled on a date for a cruise. I wonder what time they'll return."

"I'm sorry, I don't know, but I would think they'd be here by late afternoon. I'm sure the shops close earlier on Sunday."

"Yeah, well I guess I'll go on to church, then. I can check back after lunch and see if she's here. It's our regular day to go to lunch. Maybe I'll give her a call."

"I noticed earlier that she left her phone on the kitchen counter." Jude was staring at Barry, wondering if she should offer him something to drink. It was awkward, since it was a house he was much more familiar with than her. He seemed perturbed that Birdie wasn't there and that he didn't know her plans. Jude thought he was more handsome than the photo on his book. She stammered and fumbled with Ollie's leash, not knowing what else to say to him.

"Well, when Birdie gets back, I'll let her know you came by. I'm sure it just slipped her mind. She was a little, I don't know, anxious about the shopping trip and preoccupied."

"Uh, can we talk for a few minutes? Barry said.

"Sure. Can I get you some coffee?"

Jude poured them both mugs from the warm pot still sitting under the coffee maker, and they followed Ollie onto the back porch. Barry was worried about Birdie taking the pills that caused her to sleep when he'd called following the storm.

"I can understand that," Jude said. "I honestly think it was a fluke. The electricity was out, and she got up during the night to take an aspirin and got the bottles mixed up. She was embarrassed by it, really."

Barry glanced around the porch. Jude thought he was needlessly worried about the incident, and he seemed overly cautious. "How well do you know Birdie?" Barry asked.

"We've known each other maybe a week. I think it'll be a week tomorrow. I've lost track of time myself. I was just thinking about the remarkable changes in weather since I've been here."

"You seem like a nice enough person," Barry began. "My aunt is kind. She would do anything for anyone, but she's also fragile. By that I don't mean her physical health, but emotionally, mentally. She's been hospitalized a couple of times. You see, I'm watchful of any change in her routine, any sign there might be something … I don't know, out of the ordinary. This situation here is certainly a change in her routine, and now you tell me she's shopping and planning a cruise."

"I consider these things healthy for a woman her age. I had to encourage her to keep the shopping plans. She wanted to back out. She's going to pick up a couple of things for the cruise." Jude was hesitant to mention that the cruise was scheduled for the next Sunday. Barry was talking like it might be a pipe dream.

"Actually, Barry, the timing of Birdie finding me on the beach was perfect, because the cruise is next week and I'll be house-sitting to water the plants and care for Ollie."

"Well, I suppose that works out for both of you, then," he stammered. "I don't know. This is just all so strange for some reason."

"I agree the situation is a little odd. Birdie and I haven't really known each other very long, but we do enjoy each other. She's like the mother I never experienced. I'm enjoying her. I appreciate her generosity and, well, I've grown to care for her in this short time.

"I've noticed a moodiness. Nothing worrisome, just a general apathy sometimes. I can usually talk her into some activity to change her attitude." Jude wanted to assure Barry that Birdie was not emotionally distraught.

"Your presence does seem to be good for her. I worry about her being in this house by herself. It does help that everyone in the neighborhood knows her situation."

"What is her situation?" Jude asked

"Aunt Birdie's always been a little off, not exactly going by the expectations of my grandparents or the rest of the family. She was a loner growing up, according to my dad. She had opportunities she didn't take advantage of, preferring to befriend people of a ... I guess you'd call it lower status than she was. She was prone to emotional outbursts as a girl, and she'd leave the house for hours, and no one knew where she was.

"She did go to college, but while she was there she had a severe breakdown, one she couldn't recover from, and she was hospitalized. According to my dad, she wouldn't talk to him or my grandparents, even after she was released from the hospital. From then on, she was pretty much treated as a fragile person, unable to finish school, work, or make her own way. Dad did mention that my grandparents thought they knew what was wrong with her, and they asked the preacher to work with her, but I never put much stock in their efforts there. I couldn't see where they would get the ideas they had." Barry waved his hand, a dismissive gesture Jude didn't question.

Jude found it hard to believe that anyone would consider Birdie unemployable. She was witty, could carry on intelligent conversations, and was well groomed. Jude couldn't see any of the things Barry described in Birdie. She wondered at his description of Birdie befriending people of "lower status." Was that supposed to include her? Was Birdie known for bringing home strays who would then take advantage of her? Jude wasn't sure where she fit in Barry's concerns.

They finished their coffee and Barry promised to check with Birdie later in the day. He stood at the front door to leave, then turned to her. "Oh, I meant to ask, what do you do, Jude? I mean for employment?"

"I have a degree in graphic design. My plans were interrupted, so I intend to research what I can find online to work virtually from here. When Birdie returns from her trip, I'll reevaluate my living situation. Maybe I'll check out what's available in Houston or return to Austin."

"And your family?"

"I don't really have a family. I grew up in several foster homes. I have siblings somewhere, which is another project I want to tackle—searching for them."

"Hmm, sorry about that. Okay, tell Birdie I'll be in touch later."

Jude closed the door before he could turn again, anxious for him to leave. She didn't want to hear anything else about Birdie. His probing questions irritated her. She collected the coffee mugs and took them to the kitchen sink. Ollie stood at her feet, waiting for his morning treat.

"Of course, sorry, Ollie. He disrupted our morning, didn't he?" She delivered Ollie's treat, continuing to be preoccupied by Barry's comments. Maybe she fit the pitiful description of derelicts Birdie might befriend.

Except for a short break for lunch, Jude spent the rest of the morning and part of the afternoon creating the sea glass jewelry for Birdie. She had purchased a small gift box and ribbon to wrap them in for presentation. After she finished, Jude was anxious for Birdie to return. She wanted to see Birdie's purchases and present her with the jewelry.

Birdie's phone rang and Jude noticed the call was from Barry. She answered and told him Birdie wasn't home yet. He said he planned to return to Houston, but to be sure and tell Birdie he came by. Jude thought it was odd that Barry's admissions did nothing to sway her loyalty to Birdie. If anything, it made her like Birdie more.

CHAPTER 25

BIRDIE

BIRDIE'S HEAD BOBBED as she fought to remain alert in the back seat. The sun shone on her, and the movement lulled her into a nap. The trunk of the car was full of bags and boxes of shoes tied with colorful ribbon. Everyone was pleased with their finds. Birdie had accomplished all of her goals, and she was anxious to show Jude the beautiful silk caftan.

The clerk helped Birdie find the perfect scarf by rummaging through the clearance bin. It had the exact colors she needed and was a generous oversized wrap. The sales lady assured Birdie that their cashmere blend scarves seldom made their way to the clearance table. It was a stroke of luck. She had been tempted to wrap it around her shoulders and wear it out of the boutique.

Birdie saw glimpses of Jude sitting on the hanging bed with her laptop as they pulled up in front of the house. Jude stood and waved from the porch, then motioned to Ollie to stay while she walked to the car to help Birdie with the bags from the trunk. He obeyed and waited on the top step. Birdie introduced Jude to Maxine, Betty, and Loretta as her new friend and house sitter. She thanked them for a lovely outing and waved them off, promising to call Maxine during the week to confirm their departure plans.

"Well, I'm happy that's done," Birdie sighed. "I got some lovely things, Jude. Just what we talked about and a few more small items, a cute bag to throw over my shoulder for excursions and some flats that caught my eye. It really was more fun than I anticipated. Thanks for encouraging me to go."

They chatted about their brunch, the items the other ladies found, and Jude mentioned Barry's visit.

"It dawned on me this might be the day he came. He never really lets me know ahead of time. Thing is, I think he just always expects me to be here. Well, serves him right to find me away from home, not waiting for him."

"He didn't know about the cruise, Birdie."

"Oh, I've talked with him about it. He just didn't believe I'd actually follow through with going. What else did he say?"

"He just asked that I let you know he came by and that he would talk with you later. You might give him a call and let him know you're home."

"If I think about it later, I will. I'm going to get these things out and packed first."

Birdie ruminated about what else Barry might have mentioned to Jude. He was prone to be rude with his probing. Birdie often accused his lawyer training for his blunt questioning. She didn't want him to come across too possessive, and he might have been so about her or the house. That was her only regret about him finding Jude there alone. She had faith that Jude could handle the situation, but she wasn't sure about Barry.

"How was Barry when he was here earlier? Did he seem okay?"

"Yes, he was fine," Jude said. "Has he been sick?"

"No, I just wondered if he was polite and friendly. I thought he might be perturbed with me for not telling him I would be out."

"Well, he was a little disappointed that he wouldn't get to see you, but other than that he was fine."

"You wouldn't bullshit me, would you?" Birdie said, her hand firmly on her hip.

Jude laughed. "Birdie, he was quite gracious. He obviously cares about you and was looking forward to seeing you. He's more handsome than that picture on the back of his book. If I were you, I'd be a little disappointed to not be escorted to church with him this morning."

"That's all his idea, not mine. I've never really told him how I feel about those compulsory Sunday morning trips to church. I've never really felt compelled to do it unless he made a point of it. I do it out of duty, not desire. I made peace with myself long ago, or at least I think I did."

"You do it out of duty to him. That's sweet, Birdie. You don't want to hurt his feelings."

"Yeah, I suppose. What else did he say about me?"

"He wasn't here that long. I told you everything he said."

Birdie doubted what Jude was telling her. She knew how he was, how her whole family had been. They thought she was a ticking time bomb, ready to go off. They never understood her angst when she was a young woman, the turmoil locked inside her. She somehow worked her way through that period only to be dealt the ultimate blow, but she had since decided she could stuff those feelings in a corner of herself, a place she would allow to wither. She knew Barry was waiting for those emotions to overpower her. She felt it. He would surely mention it to Jude, and if he did, it would be her opportunity to tell Jude the truth.

"I know Barry. He's like the rest of my family, all about appearances. He walks on pins and needles, worried I'll spoil the family name. He likes to dress up and take me to church, smiling at the people who do the same. They say hello and repeat the same words every time I see them, but there's nothing beyond that, beyond those faces. It's hollow."

"I don't think that's fair, Birdie. I read Barry's book. It seemed sincere and insightful to me."

"There are people who make excellent presentations, and I should know. I'm one of them. I can pretend to be something I'm not."

"Birdie, I find you genuine. I've only known you for a short time, and I think you can be moody and inclined to shy away from other people, but your interactions with me have been genuine. Is there something about you I should know?"

Birdie wasn't going to answer that honestly, or maybe it was honest to say no. How could she possibly judge what Jude should or shouldn't know? Her head hurt thinking about it, and it was of no consequence one way or the other, so she said, "No. I'm an open book, don't you think? Now, tell me what you're doing on that laptop."

"I do have some news about that. You're right, you do have excellent Wi-Fi reception here. I've secured a few projects for graphic design that I can work on from here. One of them offers a possibility for regular, ongoing work if they like what I do on the first job."

"That's great news. Of all things. Isn't that something? The world has really changed. You don't even have to leave the house to do meaningful work. If that had been available when I was young, I could've been a productive citizen." Birdie was pleased to hear that Jude could work while house-sitting, but she didn't mean to reveal the part about her own work history. She wished she could take it back.

"Tell me more about what you'll be doing." Birdie said, trying to give Jude little time to think about her last comment.

Jude helped Birdie pack her new purchases while explaining what work she would be doing for her new clients. She had prepared a quiche to pop in the oven later for supper so Birdie could relax from the day of shopping. Jude's thoughtfulness delighted Birdie. She spied a salad, covered and waiting to be dressed, in the refrigerator.

Birdie let Ollie out the back door, following him with a glass of wine. She had forgotten how exhausting a day of shopping could be. It felt good to put her feet up and sit with the Sunday crossword puzzle while Ollie roamed in the courtyard. She put Barry's visit out of her mind until she called him later. Birdie intended to question him about his conversation with Jude. She wouldn't let him control everything about her life.

The folded paper and pen were in Birdie's lap, her mind wandering as she sipped the wine. She was having a flashback to the feeling she would get when her parents questioned her about why she couldn't follow through with her responsibilities as a debutant. She felt as if her body sat motionless while her head slowly evaporated from her shoulders. She caught parts of the sentences, responsibilities, why, wrong .... The words were meaningless because she couldn't define herself in their world. She would leave, walking to join Henry on the beach. She walked without her head—erased by her parents. It would slowly reappear when Henry arrived. Then there could be tears and words that made sense and real shoes on her feet and sips of beer.

Henry said, "Don't worry, this isn't important. When it's over, they'll forget about it and it'll be a thing in the past to laugh about, a memory to share about Birdie being Birdie."

But Birdie knew it was a symptom of something else. She was disappearing, and soon there would be no shoulders or arms. They were erasing her and trying to replace her with a girl in a gown, a smiling girl, bowing to the others, someone she didn't know.

CHAPTER 26

JUDE

THE TABLE WAS set and Jude glanced onto the porch to see
Birdie sitting with a glass of wine, working the puzzles in the
paper. She took the quiche out of the oven. The small box with
the sea glass jewelry was set at Birdie's place. Jude tossed the
salad and placed it on the table before taking her wine and
joining Birdie on the porch.

"I can hear a train," Jude said. "Where's that coming from?"

"On days when the wind is from the north, the sounds carry.
It's nice, isn't it, to be able to hear a train?"

"This is the first time I noticed."

"Sometimes I notice," Birdie said. "Most of the time I take
it for granted. Trains remind me of my childhood. I'd ride my
bike across Broadway to 'backtrack.' My parents never knew I
was going over there. Not many white children went that far,

but my friend Henry lived there, and we would go exploring by the warehouses. Those were the good old days. You met Eldon. He and Henry were cousins. They were always together. I envied them having a cousin to be with all the time."

Birdie sat staring out at the garden. Jude thought the wine was allowing her to reminisce. "We could say anything to each other, anything. It was always okay. No matter what it was, we always knew it would be okay. We ate sardines from the can, sardines packed in mustard. I can still taste them. I can smell the warehouse and hear the trains pulling up. The sounds shook the buildings."

Jude watched Birdie's face as she got lost in the sounds and smells of the warehouse she described. Her eyes became glassy. Jude was awed by Birdie traveling back in time, aware of the details of her childhood.

"My parents would say it wasn't safe to ride my bike down there. They would caution me never to do it again and threaten to take my bike away. It was the safest place I've ever been, the most comfortable, where I could be myself." Birdie stopped talking, her face calm with memories.

"All the remembrances I have of Henry are special. I can hear those coupling contraptions making those awful metal noises. We held our ears and squealed at the top of our lungs.

The noise was deafening. It was like the relief of strenuous exercise to yell while the trains reverberated past the warehouse.

"Henry made up a murder mystery while we sat there. He would recite a few scenes and then save the rest of the story for our next visit. I couldn't get to backtrack fast enough to hear the next segment of his story. That was his gift, to tell stories and take me to another place. I always wanted to hear Henry talk."

"The quiche is ready when you are," Jude said.

"It smells delicious, and I'm ready." Birdie followed Jude into the kitchen. "Oh, look at this. It's not my birthday."

Jude smiled. "I don't even know when your birthday is, Birdie. I'll have to find out. That's just a little something I thought you might want to pack for the cruise." Jude watched Birdie's face light up as she anticipated the surprise.

"Can I open it now?"

"Sure, go ahead, and I'll cut the quiche."

"Oh, how lovely. I can't believe you've already created this jewelry. They're perfect." Birdie held the earrings up to her ears and walked to the mirror in the den to look at herself. "They look good with my gray hair, don't you think?" Birdie peered around the wall and smiled at Jude. Her eyes twinkled. She attached the pin to her top and patted it, taking her place at the table.

"Yes, I imagined they would. I suspected those frosty colors would bring out your eyes and hair."

"Thank you so much. They're perfect. I think I'll wear them to get on the boat. That way I won't have to pack them. They'll be perfect with my outfit.

"You're so talented, Jude, a good cook, an accomplished artist, master packer, and jewelry maker—so many skills. You're a remarkable young woman."

Jude blushed. "I never thought about it, but I guess I take those things for granted. I just did things growing up because there was often no one else to do them."

"Lots of people do things, but you make an effort to do them well. I don't think that's common."

"I never thought about not doing the best I could do," Jude said. "I always wanted people to like me, so I did my best to show them I was likeable. It was part of moving from family to family and trying to earn a place at the table, I guess."

"You don't have to do that here, you know. I'm easily impressed. I'm just afraid you'll tire of me and Ollie and pack up and leave while we're enjoying your company."

"Oh, I didn't mean to suggest that. I made dinner because I wanted to. I thought you might be tired from shopping. The ingredients were here, and I had the time on my hands, so I just thought it would be good to prepare something. My job search went smoother than I anticipated. I thought I might be at that for hours."

Jude's thoughts went back to Birdie's earlier comments about being a productive citizen. She hoped she hadn't reopened a wound. She didn't like having to pick and choose her words. Barry's earlier remarks were on her mind. She was also thinking about Birdie's boast that she and Henry and Eldon could say anything to each other. She seemed to appreciate the ability to be totally honest. Birdie was a puzzle Jude couldn't figure out.

"I really didn't intend to imply that I was trying to keep my place at your table, Birdie. I don't feel like that's necessary. I feel welcome here, I really do."

"You are welcome, Jude. I wasn't thinking otherwise. I was just making a joke. Sometimes my jokes fall flat. Have you noticed? I stick my foot in my mouth sometimes, always have."

Jude laughed. "We all do that, Birdie. It's not just you—" Jude stopped. Her head tilted and she looked toward the front door.

"What's the matter?" Birdie asked.

"Nothing, I thought it was that motorcycle."

"Tell me why you're afraid of that," Birdie insisted, putting her fork down and wiping her lips with the napkin. "You turn pale and retreat when you hear a motorcycle. Is it Jax?"

"Yes, it's Jax. I'm afraid he's still out there, looking for me."

"Why would that be? He's done the damage he wanted to do. He's stopped Casey, stopped her adventure and ended her life. What else would he be doing?

"He wants to stop me. I'm sure he does. I was … well, I was the one taking Casey away from him."

"Nonsense." Birdie rolled her eyes. "You're just imagining things. You need to release that fear, Jude. I'm sure he's gone back to Austin, and the police are certainly looking for him. Eldon took that information. He should be easy to find. You've said you suspected he was involved in other illegal activities."

"It haunts me." Jude put her fork down, having lost her appetite. She couldn't finish the quiche, so Jude took her plate to the sink and scraped the food into the garbage disposal. She closed her eyes as she listened to the grinding motor and the running water. The noise threatened to carry her away. She wanted the thoughts of Jax and his menacing to disappear. He would be a threat to her until someone could tell her he was put away.

Birdie couldn't know how he felt about Jude, and she didn't know how to explain it. She wanted to tell Birdie, but she was afraid Birdie wouldn't understand. There was no need to tell her. It wasn't important.

"I'll do the dishes, Jude. You cooked. Take your wine and go out there on the porch and relax. I'll finish up in here."

Jude did as Birdie suggested. It wasn't just Jax that was turning her stomach. It had been a bad day as far as her stomach was concerned. There had been bad days before, but she brushed them off. Now she knew what the problem was. She found out when she was in the emergency room for the two days after the accident. It was confirmed.

Jude put that bit of information out of her mind. She didn't intend to worry about it for a while. She had time to decide. Maybe after Birdie returned from her cruise, they could talk. It would be nice to have another opinion about what she should do.

CHAPTER 27

BIRDIE

AFTER FALLING INTO bed, certain she would be asleep before her head hit the pillow, Birdie could not shut her mind off. She thought about the day shopping with her friends. She was bothered about Barry's visit, wondering if Jude had told her everything. Barry tended to be overly concerned about her business, and she was sure he was peeved that he didn't know she had finalized plans for the cruise. It would be considerate if he would call the day before he intended to make a trip to the island to find out if she would be available.

Birdie also thought about her conversation with Jude. She had sympathy for her as a child growing up in other people's homes—homes where she wasn't sure she belonged. It must've been difficult for her. Birdie tried to imagine it, but she had no frame of reference. Her own parents were always so hands on, maybe too much so. They didn't always know where she was, but that was her trying to avoid them.

Jude was still on alert about Casey's boyfriend. Birdie was hopeful that Eldon could give them some news on whether he had been apprehended.

After all the anxious thoughts, Birdie settled in and remembered thinking about the sardines in mustard she had shared with Henry in the float warehouses. They sat between the floats, listening for any sounds they didn't recognize. Sometimes there would be big rats running along the walls and under the floats. They were careful not to disturb the colorful decorations.

For Henry, the ornate trailers were part of the parades for two weeks during Mardi Gras, but for Birdie they were the obsession of her parents and members of their krewe. They would be the people atop the structures, throwing beads into the crowds and waving. Henry and his family would be standing on the street or running alongside, their arms raised and voices pleading, catching the beads.

Birdie was struck every year by the disconnect between her parents and her best friend. She couldn't bridge the chasm between them. Neither could fit themselves into the world of the other, nor did they have the desire. Birdie wondered why she loved them all and why she had the impossible yearning to see them together. She wondered, but she knew the answer. Birdie had never been one to accept things as they were. She was different, and she was convinced that no one could possibly be as different or understand the way it felt.

Henry shook his head often, telling her that she had no idea how many people were different and had the same feelings. He laughed at Birdie and told her she just wanted to feel special about it, but she wasn't special; she was just like everyone else. She thought too hard about it instead of living it. Birdie remembered Henry said it was just something to get through.

Birdie never knew what that meant. She wasn't sure if Henry knew what he was talking about, but he made her feel better on the hardest days. Sometimes he would get angry when she would complain. "Fuck sakes, Birdie. You're white. Your parents have plenty of money. You live in that big house. You'll go to college. What do you have to worry about?"

Henry was right. She had all the advantages—that was the problem. Maybe if she didn't have to worry about the status of her parents, she could've been more comfortable with herself. She had wanted to rebel, but she wasn't any good at it. She was chicken. In her family it wasn't okay for the females to be rebellious, but it was okay for them to be sick, or overwrought, or nervous. They couldn't be tenacious or headstrong, so Birdie feigned illness to avoid the things her parents pushed on her.

Birdie remembered the day of the formal ball. She had already told her mother she was feeling weak and headachy. They had spent thousands on deposits, parties, gowns, and their own clothing. Friends had planned parties, teas, and luncheons. There were dark ink marks on the calendar hanging on the refrigerator. They hung there, unfading. They haunted Birdie's weekend for over six months. Everything from November through Fat Tuesday was dedicated to the season of the debutant. She forced herself to accompany her mother to the minor events, but she had no intention of following through to the climax.

After her family left the house, her parents dressed in their formal attire and Pete in his tux with a corsage for his date, Birdie stared from under the covers at the deep purple gown hanging on the front of her closet door. It was a gown designed just for her. She had hung the matching mask, studded with sparkling rhinestones, from a nail on her wall. Gold ribbons hung from the mask almost touching the floor. It was fastened to a wand laced with purple, green and gold ribbon. She was instructed to hold the wand high in the air as she leaned into the deep bow.

Birdie admired the colors in the mask and thought it would have been wonderful to hide her face behind it. She got up from her bed and slipped into the gown. She stood in front of her full length mirror, holding the mask in her hand. They wanted her to be seen on the stage in the beautiful dress. That's all they wanted, but she couldn't do it.

The phone rang. Birdie tossed the mask on her bed and went into the hall. It was Henry's cousin, Silvie.

"Birdie, I knew you'd want to know. Aunt Mary had a visit this afternoon from some soldiers. I'm sorry, Birdie. Henry has passed. They said he was a hero."

She dropped the phone and walked back into her room. She broke the wand from the mask and tied it across her face. Birdie didn't bother to put her shoes on. Parade attendees on the seawall recalled seeing a girl in a beautiful purple gown riding a bicycle with gold ribbons trailing behind her. They thought she was part of the spectacle. Pete found her, hours later, standing on the beach facing the water. She didn't speak for days and when she did, she asked Pete who he danced with at the ball.

In Harvey and Maudine Barnes's minds, their daughter was a debutant. But, Birdie was Birdie Barnes, friend of Henry, half-hearted student, miserable daughter, and lipstick lesbian. There, she admitted it, finally said what Henry had been begging her to tell herself until the day he died. She was a doily dyke, living her life as a lie, trying to be someone she wasn't.

Birdie said those things in her head, in her own thoughts, as she rolled over and looked at the ceiling. From her bed, she felt the heaviness of the house. The air in the room grew thick around her. She needed to create some movement or she could suffocate. She had broken into a sweat, and her body was clammy. Birdie slid out of bed and flicked the switch to start the ceiling fan, then took a sip of water from the glass on her bedside table. Standing by the bed, she looked at the rumpled sheets in the gray light from the windows. She pulled the fitted sheet tight and tucked it under the mattress, then smoothed the top sheet flat and turned it down.

It was a milestone—Birdie had crossed the invisible barrier, the obstacle that kept her from accepting and sharing herself with others. In one moment, it was a terrific burden, and in the next breath it was the relief she had longed for. Tears came to her eyes when she thought about how stubborn she had been and how proud Henry would be.

In some ways, Birdie thought all Henry ever wanted was for her to say it aloud so he could hear it. She knew he could hear even though she still hadn't said it aloud. Then it dawned on her, as clearly as if the son of God stood in front of her and said the words. Birdie heard the truth—Henry was asleep upstairs, in the guest room. Of course he was. It couldn't be anyone else. If she had uttered a prayer in all the years since his passing, that was it. So there he was, his undying spirit returned to her, accepting her, and encouraging her to live the authentic life she was meant to live.

Birdie took another sip of water, then crawled in bed. The air moved around her, whispering through her hair. Her eyes were heavy, and the air was light. Cool air breathed on her skin. She sank into her bed, aware of the comfort of the sheets. She was swaddled by the truth she'd accepted. It comforted her to know that she could be exactly who she was, and no one could make her do anything she didn't want to do. Birdie Barnes was born, delivered from the staleness of restless sleep into the comfort of knowing who she was.

She closed her eyes. Her last thought before she drifted into dreams was that she would still be there in the morning—the real Birdie, the one she longed to introduce to her parents, her brother, and Barry. The Birdie Henry had always known, the one he begged her to be.

"Do you believe in reincarnation, Jude?" Birdie asked when Jude came down the next morning for breakfast.

"It's funny you ask that," Jude said, pouring herself a mug of coffee. "Just before we left Austin, I had finished a book. Casey and I talked about it on the drive down here. It had been something I developed an interest in when it was brought up in an anthropology class. I had always wanted to do more reading on it, and I finally did. I don't know if it fits in my belief system, but it makes sense in the grand scheme of things."

"I had an epiphany in my restless thoughts before falling asleep last night. You're going to think I'm a crazy old woman. Maybe I am. I've known since I found you on the beach that you're someone from my past to lead me to my future. You can't convince me otherwise. I know exactly who you are. You don't fool me for a minute."

Jude smiled, looking at Birdie over the rim of the coffee mug. "You've figured this all out, the fact that we've had this coincidental meeting and bonding experience?" Jude grinned. "This came to you in a shaft of light during the night?"

"You scoff, but that's exactly what happened."

"So who am I, Birdie?"

"You know exactly who you are. It doesn't matter that you have a different name. Your spirit is here, and I've always known it. It could've passed me by without me recognizing. That would've been an easy thing to do, but I bet you'd have come back for me. Somehow, you would've. I appreciate that you did. I truly do."

Jude seemed confused by Birdie's sudden epiphany, but Birdie didn't care. She knew she was right. "There are so many things I've wanted to do but I've put them off, not knowing if I should move forward with any of my decisions. From now on, I'm going to trust my instincts and do what I have the urge to do. One thing I'm going to get to is painting the living and dining area. I bought the paint a long time ago, but it's just been sitting out there in the garage. It may have dried up by now. I've always wanted those rooms to be brighter. I think I'd use them more."

Birdie sighed. She thought saying it aloud would actually make her follow through with the plan.

Jude smiled at her new enthusiasm. Birdie definitely woke up on the right side of the bed.

CHAPTER 28

JUDE

IT WAS ENTERTAINING to listen to Birdie talk about her epiphany; however, Jude had no idea what she meant. All she knew was she was glad Birdie's spirit was lifted.

Birdie had clipped zinnias from the garden and placed them in a vase on the kitchen table. Cloth napkins were at their places. Birdie was dressed for the day, not in her gown and robe, and she had applied lipstick.

Jude had only one regret about the morning. The pills they gave her in the emergency room were no longer providing much relief. Her stomach continued to ache. She found little comfort as she squirmed in the wicker chair on the porch.

Birdie looked up from her crossword puzzle. "Is something bothering you, Jude? Does your back hurt?"

"No, just a little stomachache. It'll pass."

"I have some Pepto, you want some?"

"No, thanks. I've already taken something. It'll be okay."

Birdie put the paper to the side. "Why don't you go back to bed. I can take Ollie for a walk, and then I'll make you some of that tea that's supposed to relax stomach pain."

"I think I'll do that, Birdie. Maybe if I go back to bed, it'll give the medicine I've taken a chance to work."

Birdie gathered the leash and keys, and she and Ollie headed out the door. Ollie glance back at Jude as if to ask why she wasn't coming, or maybe he knew her pain and he said something. He did say something, something he wanted her to understand, but she couldn't quite make it out. She thought he said "thank you," and something about Birdie.

Jude pulled her hair back and held it at her neck with her elbows in the air as she watched them from the door. She closed her eyes and waited for a wave of pain to subside. Jude glanced toward the stairs, but she didn't think she could make her way back to the guest room. She walked onto the porch and headed to the hanging bed. It was around the corner, hidden a bit. After she was settled, Jude could hear the surf and the rhythm of the traffic on the seawall. She allowed the gentle swaying of the bed and the white noise to take her to another place, a place with no pain. She practiced the meditations she had learned in her previous yoga classes.

Jude saw herself sitting on the beach with Birdie. They were talking. Ollie wasn't there. She knew it was Birdie, but Birdie was a younger version of herself. Jude was slightly younger but not much. She noticed her hands were black. She wore khaki pants and high-top tennis shoes. Jude knew it was her. She knew the feelings, and she knew Birdie. *I'm supposed to tell Birdie something, something to make her feel better.* Jude knew Birdie wouldn't listen. Well, she might listen, but she wouldn't hear.

Birdie cried, unable to resolve the feelings she was experiencing, and Jude couldn't understand what could possibly be so upsetting. Then, as she was listening, Jude heard it—the one thing that made it different. She heard the thing that no one could help Birdie resolve.

I'm black, Jude thought. *My mother, my cousins, my father, I think. We're all black. Some of us are lighter, some darker, but we're all black. With the exception of the people on Aunt Peaches's side—we still like them—we're all black. Birdie is the only one like her in her family. Maybe her mother, her father, her brother don't like people like her. They don't accept that she could be different from them, not the same. Birdie won't know unless she tells them, and she's afraid to tell them.*

Jude told Birdie that she could tell her parents. She could tell them she was different. If they loved her, they would accept her, though they might need her to help them. It wouldn't be easy, but they could all get through it together.

Birdie listened, but she doubted what she was hearing. Jude could tell by looking at her, she wasn't convinced.

Jude opened her eyes. She wasn't sure how much time had passed, but the aching in her stomach was gone. She was under a quilt she didn't remember. Jude rolled off the bed and stood, still wearing the T-shirt and yoga pants she'd slept in. She looked at her hands. They were white with the nail polish she'd chosen for her manicure. She couldn't remember what she'd dreamed, but she thought she'd dreamed she was black.

When Jude entered the house, she could hear Birdie talking to Ollie from the back porch. She went to the French doors and Birdie turned and looked toward her. "I'm sorry, did I wake you? Ollie and I tried not to disturb you. You were sleeping so soundly. He has a squirrel cornered. They're having a stand-off down there. How's your stomach?"

"It's perfect. Good as new. I was just going to rest there for a few minutes. I must have dozed. I'm going up to put on my clothes for the day."

"Sure thing. I'm going to walk around the corner to the market. If you need something, I'll be happy to pick it up."

"I'm good, Birdie. I don't need a thing, but thanks."

Jude heard Birdie go out the front door. As she stepped into the shower, she closed her eyes and tipped her head back, feeling the steam rise around her. There was something about her dream that she wanted to remember, something about Birdie. She reached for the places in her mind that could take her to the dream again, but she couldn't find it.

As she tried to relax her shoulders and allow her mind to drift, thoughts of Ollie telling her "thank you" kept popping up. The words were written in black behind her closed eyes. They floated there, not letting her reach her dream.

CHAPTER 29

BIRDIE

THE MARKET WAS quiet. Birdie thought she might be the only shopper. She gathered items to make soup for dinner and carbonated sodas. Jude's stomach problems were a source of worry. Birdie thought she might be losing weight. It was hard to tell, since she had only known her less than two weeks, but she imagined there were circles under Jude's eyes that weren't there before.

Birdie appreciated that the produce in their neighborhood grocery was locally grown and fresh. Her handbasket was overflowing with carrots with feathery green tops, purple new potatoes, celery, and hand-packed bags of pasta. She had a boiling chicken thawing and would make her favorite open-faced grilled cheese. She picked up a bottle of white wine.

"How you doing, Birdie? I haven't seen you since the storm. Did you weather that okay?"

"Did just fine, George. Thank you for asking. How much are those orchids outside?"

"I'll throw one in for you, Birdie. Joe ordered those, and I don't think I can keep them alive so I'm trying to get rid of them."

"Well, of course I'll take one. The price is right."

"You on foot? This is going to be a heavy haul. Let me get Joe to deliver this to your house. We're slow this afternoon. He'll be there in the next thirty minutes."

"Mighty fine. Thank you, George. That kind of service keeps me coming back. I appreciate it."

"No problem, Birdie. Always happy to see you."

Birdie left the market with no bags, feeling almost lighter than when she went in. She avoided the alley and walked down the street, noting some of the yards still had branches that had blown down during the storm. Some houses had their storm blinds rolled down. She suspected some of her neighbors had left and not yet returned.

She turned down a street where the houses looked different. She was noticing details she hadn't seen before.

It seemed like the storm had taken place a long time ago. She marked time by the event. That's when Jude arrived.

Although it hadn't really been that long, there were times when she and Jude were talking when she had a sense they'd had the discussion before, déjà vu. Other times, Birdie thought she didn't know the young woman at all, more a stranger than a friend.

It made no sense to Birdie now that she ever considered Jude might have Henry's soul. Was that a foggy thought resulting from a dream, or could it be possible? Nothing in her upbringing ever made her consider that souls could be reincarnated, that she could have the opportunity to know someone more than once. Where in the world would that notion originate? *You are a silly old woman, Birdie, losing your marbles.*

But it was so real. That would be miraculous if Henry could talk with her another time, if they could have the conversations she'd looked forward to when she was isolated in the middle of her family. He knew how she felt, knew her isolation. If Jude could have his soul, she would be enchanted. It would fit. It shouldn't be impossible, but it would fit.

Birdie continued to walk, the houses had been painted different colors since the last time she had been down that street. Trees and new plantings changed the appearance. When she reached the corner, the street sign was gone. She looked up through the canopy of oak branches to see the sun directly overhead, but what direction had she walked? Birdie's heart began to race as she looked right and then left. There was no indication of which way the water would be. She stood still and listened, but she couldn't hear the surf. Maybe she had walked north.

Cars were driving by, going faster than usual in her little neighborhood. It was as if it was a major thoroughfare, not her area at all. *I left that silly phone at home again.* Birdie chose to turn left, going the direction of most of the traffic. She thought the cars must be going toward the seawall, but the more she walked, she could see the esplanade and the trees. It was Broadway. Finally, she reached a street sign. She was two blocks too far west and seven blocks too far north. *Oh, for Pete's sake.*

When Birdie finally arrived home, the groceries had been delivered and Jude was beside herself with worry about where Birdie might've been. Birdie was relieved to be home, but she didn't want to admit her foolish error. *It had been a foolish error, hadn't it?*

"I walked a different route. There have been so many pleasant changes, I kept walking to bring myself up to date. It was a great day for it. I'm sorry I worried you, Jude."

"You didn't take your phone, Birdie. I didn't know how to reach you."

"Oh, I can't get used to it, carrying that damn thing everywhere I go. You don't understand. This technology has taken me by surprise, and it's such a burden sometimes. I had just gotten used to the damn answering machine, but all of a sudden you could carry everything in your pocket and take pictures with it, too. It's just too much to remember."

Jude laughed and continued to giggle as she and Birdie unpacked the groceries. Birdie held the orchid up and said, "Look what George gave me for shopping today."

"He gave that to you? It's lovely."

"Yeah, I liked it, so he gave it to me." Birdie put the plant in the center of the kitchen table. "I have lots of friends in this neighborhood. I was just thinking that while I was walking around."

"You do. In the short time I've been here, that's the one thing that stands out to me, Birdie. Everyone loves you. They've known you all your life. They knew your parents. They know Barry, and they love you."

"So here it comes again." Birdie turned toward Jude with her hands on her hips. Her eyes began to get misty as she stared at Jude, looking directly in her eyes. "Why did you have to come here to remind me of that? You're here for a reason. You're Jude, but you know that 'hey' part, that's for me. It's to get my attention."

"I don't know what you're talking about, Birdie. It's not making sense to me. Did you get lost this afternoon? Are you feeling okay?"

"Hmpf. I don't know what I'm talking about either. It's magical, but I found my way home just fine."

Birdie wasn't going to admit she was afraid. She never admitted that to anyone. Well, only one person—Henry. Everyone else thought she was headstrong and fearless. She was afraid of getting lost in her own neighborhood, of taking the bow in front of all the people she had known all her life, of disappointing her parents, of losing Henry, but what she was most afraid of was losing what Jude had just reminded her she'd always had.

Jude would think she was crazy if she said it again. So she wasn't going to say it. She couldn't be crazy just now. She was going on a cruise and she needed to finish packing. Before that, she was going to make her cure-all soup and treat Jude to her famous grilled cheese.

CHAPTER 30

JUDE

BIRDIE HAD TRIED to brush it off, but Jude was certain she had become disoriented on her walk home and had been lost. If she wasn't so preoccupied by her own illness, Jude would've gone out to look for Birdie. They told her before she left the hospital that she should follow up, but the doctor also noted that there was no treatment available.

She and Casey had suspected her condition was serious, but it hadn't been confirmed when they left Austin. Casey was going to help her fulfill her bucket list before she settled down to her own life. Things certainly had a way of happening to upend all plans.

Now here she was with Birdie, a woman who was going through some sort of midlife epiphany or something, seeing Jude as a soul she knew before. Everything that had happened since she set foot on the island had upset all her plans. It was no longer about her. She was part of something grander than the plans she and Casey had made. She was on her way to something bigger than Europe

Jude sat on the porch with her computer, clicking and dragging while Birdie prepared soup in the kitchen. Ollie was curled up at Jude's feet. She had completed one project and already received payment through direct deposit in an online account. The work she had lined up was working out well, kept her focused while she was biding her time. She looked forward to house-sitting for Birdie and spending some quiet days by herself. Jude planned to do some writing. Maybe it would help her process what she was going through. She had also located the paint Birdie mentioned in the garage. Nothing soothed her more than being able to see a finished project, and painting would give her that satisfaction.

The odors of Birdie's cooking wafted to the porch, a pleasant combination of chicken stock and bread. Ollie lifted up his head and sniffed the air. Jude knew she had never eaten better food than at Birdie's. Her meals as a child had been inconsistent and marginal at best. There was no comfort in the comfort food her foster parents offered. She recalled one brief placement where the family made meals of rice flavored with pungent curry and different broths with green onion floating on top. They spoke between themselves in a language Jude didn't understand, and she often left the table unfulfilled to close herself up in a tiny bedroom.

Jude hadn't thought of the family in a long time. They smiled and nodded at her, but she couldn't recall ever touching them or having a conversation. She suspected they had called the social worker and told him the placement wasn't going to work out. She wasn't disappointed that she'd had to move for the third time; Jude agreed that the placement had little hope of being pleasant for her or the family.

Jude suspected they wanted to make a deserving child happy, and she was having difficulty presenting herself as either one. It had been Jude's experience in other homes with multiple foster children that they often weren't warm and fuzzy creatures. They had considerable baggage with known and unknown sordid histories.

The history social workers told Jude's various foster parents about her was just the CliffsNotes version of her story. Some of the details they chose to leave out but others they didn't know. Jude never told all of her story. When she did choose to share it, the listener would clutch their throat, grimace, and shake their head, often muttering, "You poor child." Jude didn't want sympathy.

Mr. and Mrs. McKnight were the only family Jude could have lived with forever. She felt comfortable in their home and genuinely loved. They weren't the typical gushy, scripture-sharing couple. Mr. McKnight was older, probably in his seventies. He was a kind man, aware of boundaries, and soft-spoken. Sitting outdoors on the back porch was his favorite pastime. He would tell stories of his childhood, growing up in the country with four brothers and two sisters. Only three of them were his natural siblings. "We are all God's children," he would say. He could twist a corn husk into the body of a doll and fold paper into little frogs and other animals.

Jude remembered keeping the small origami creatures in a drawer by her bed. They were the only things that belonged to her. Clothing and shoes were given to the foster families and were usually used items passed on to them by other people. Mr. McKnight would hand the children his creations and say, "Now, this is just for you." He somehow knew the meaning it would have.

Usually when a move was upcoming, the social worker would visit and explain when it would happen. However, after twenty-four months in the McKnight home, Mrs. McKnight entered the hospital and her sister came to help Mr. McKnight with the children. After a week, social workers began arriving to move the children to other homes. Jude regretted not being able to say goodbye to Mrs. McKnight. When she asked Mr. McKnight to say it for her, he had tears in his eyes, and Jude knew he would be telling his wife goodbye also.

Jude fit in that home. It felt like her. The common sense there was her sense. The images, the language, the smells had been soothing to her.

Jude shut down her computer and closed it, placing her hands on the laptop. She stared at her hands as she got goose bumps down her arms. They were black.

The McKnights were a black couple.

CHAPTER 31

BIRDIE

BIRDIE GLANCED OUT the door. Jude slumped with her head bent and her eyes closed. She worried Jude might be getting ill again.

"You okay, Jude?" Birdie hurried onto the porch.

Jude looked up, startled at Birdie's sudden appearance. "I'm fine. Just finished up a project."

"Oh, I was worried when I saw you with your head down. I thought maybe you were getting ill. Dinner's served."

Jude enjoyed the soup and gave Birdie heaps of compliments. As Birdie cleared the table, she said, "I'll put some in plastic containers in the freezer. You can nuke it while I'm gone."

"You're spoiling me, Birdie," Jude said, wiping her lips. "I'm not used to eating such consistently good food. Casey and I ate ramen noodles most of the time."

Birdie waited on the back porch with her luggage at her feet, dressed in white cropped pants and a light blue tunic. Her new scarf, knotted casually on the handle of a large straw bag, added just the right touch of sophistication. As she waited for Jude to help her load her bags into the car, Birdie talked with Ollie, telling him again that Jude would be keeping him company. "This is so much better than boarding, Bubba."

Maxine and Birdie chatted with excitement on the drive to the cruise terminal. Jude smiled, glancing at them. Birdie caught her look and winked at her as she touched the sea glass earring. She was looking forward to being with her friends and away from home. There was a revival in her spirit, a feeling of anticipation and a new awakening, something she hadn't felt in a long time.

Birdie thought about the phone call she'd received from Barry earlier in the morning. He was calling to wish her bon voyage and to tell her he was going to miss her. She felt guilty for not seeing him the previous Sunday. Birdie accepted that she had been hardheaded about him. *I should be grateful that I have someone who cares enough to look out for me. Some people have no one, and I have Barry and now Jude.*

Maxine told them she would be ordering one of the tall icy drinks they would serve passengers as they boarded. "It'll have a flower or umbrella sticking out of it. I don't know what they're called, but the drink of the day is what I'm going to have. I'll wear my sunglasses and walk around the decks sipping on it like I have one every afternoon." She giggled, fluffing her hair in the wind as they rode with the windows down to the ship terminal. Birdie smiled at Maxine picturing herself strolling on the deck of the big ship; they both were.

Birdie glanced in the back seat to see Maxine craning her neck to get a glimpse of the tall ship they would be boarding. Her dark, round Jackie O sunglasses were perched on her petite nose over painfully orange lips. Birdie pulled the mirror down in front of her to make sure her own lip color wasn't as glaring. She flipped it back up, confident she had made the right choice. She was equally pleased with her tortoise shell sunglasses. She could see them all walking the decks in their new outfits, leaning toward each other in conspiratorial whispers, commenting on the other passengers. It was the habit of the others to notice other people and point them out. Birdie thought she wasn't as judgmental, or she didn't want to think so.

"Oh my. Look, Maxine. They all have on those tropical shirts. Very festive," Birdie giggled. "This is going to be fun."

Stewards dressed in colorful shirts with straw hats helped Jude unload the luggage, and she hugged Maxine and Birdie before driving off. Birdie stared after the car from the sidewalk, and Maxine had to nudge her toward the registration line. "Walk on, Birdie. You're letting this crowd get ahead of us."

Now Birdie was having doubts. Jude had driven off, leaving her in front of the terminal. She had to get on the ship. There was no turning back. Suddenly she felt alone, even though Maxine was guiding her by the elbow. They were supposed to meet Betty and Loretta after they boarded. The line moved quickly, and they had their identification tags, which also served as their room key, within thirty minutes. It was a flurry of information, overwhelming Birdie.

Maxine led the way up several long ramps. They bypassed the photo opportunity and were greeted to a rush of cool air just inside the glittering lobby. Other passengers were milling around, staring up into a tall dome where glass elevators trimmed in gold were moving up and down. Waiters dressed in white jackets trimmed in gold nautical designs carried large trays with the very drinks Maxine described earlier. Maxine looped her bag over her shoulder and took a drink from the tray, handing the waiter her card to deduct the payment.

"Isn't this grand, Birdie? Look at that beautiful white piano. I bet they'll have people singing as entertainment, and there'll no doubt be couples spinning each other around on that dance floor. Get you a drink. Our adventure has begun."

"I'll pace myself, Mac. It does look inviting, but I'm not used to drinking before two in the afternoon. Just give me a minute to get acclimated. We need to take a little tour so we can get our bearings. Should we go find our rooms and see if Loretta and Betty are on board yet?"

"Yes, let's do."

They waited in a small line to take an elevator to deck eleven where they were to share a two-bedroom suite with their friends. They stood next to the glass in the carriage, peering down as they were whisked to the top floor and into bright sunlight pouring into the vaulted dome. The doors slid open, and Birdie was happy to discover the door to the suite was not far from the bank of elevators.

Birdie used her key while Maxine balanced her drink, a tote bag, and her purse. The door swung open to a wall of glass doors on the opposite side of the room, where there was a view high above the dock. They crossed the living area and stared down at the buildings.

"It looks so different from up here, doesn't it?" Maxine said.

"Yes, it's like we're not even in our own town. Look at all the bustle going on down there. I'm going to have my morning coffee out on those chairs. I don't care if the ship leaves the port. I could feel like I was on a trip parked right here."

Birdie took stock of the small common area, then looked around to find the door to their room. She looked at the number on her badge to identify which would be theirs. "It's this one." She entered the room and peeked in the bathroom. "Oh look, we have our own little balcony." It was indeed a small overhang, angled toward the larger balcony and just wide enough for two chairs and a small table. Because of the angle, it was shaded and Birdie thought very pleasant.

"I'm not mad at anybody," Maxine announced, smiling.

"Me either," Birdie agreed. She had decided she could do this. It would be fine.

Their luggage had not yet been delivered to the room. As they walked back into the common area, they could hear people exiting the elevator and chatting to get their sense of direction. Birdie walked over and closed the door, discovering they couldn't hear the noise when the door was closed. Maxine sat on the sofa and sipped her drink, looking through a printed paper with the times of the events for the day. It wasn't long before there was a knock on the door and their luggage was delivered.

As they were unpacking and chatting in their own room, Loretta and Betty arrived. They, too, were pleased with the suite and the view of the harbor. Birdie noted the time for the safety drill before they left their suite and made their way to a lounge on a lower deck to sit and gaze at the buildings in downtown Galveston. *It's a picturesque place. I take it for granted. I think we all do.*

CHAPTER 32

JUDE

WHEN JUDE RETURNED to the house, Ollie met her at the door. She attached his leash, and they left for an afternoon walk on the beach. She was relaxed and had no stomach pain. Since she had the responsibility of Ollie and felt an obligation to Birdie, she was relieved. Maybe it had been temporary and wouldn't repeat.

It was a clear, crisp day. She enjoyed the lower humidity. The Gulf water looked blue and the sun glistened, making sparkles that caused Jude to squint and look away. She thought about Birdie and her friends enjoying the water from their balcony on the ship. She could imagine them chatting and giggling. They should enjoy being together. There was something that happened when women could sit in their pajamas and enjoy each other. It was different than when they were perfumed and bedecked for their weekly games. Pretenses and defenses were let down. Birdie needed that relief.

Jude remembered the times she was able to escape the family common areas with a fellow foster child to relax in their own private space and talk about their experiences. It was sometimes comforting to be able to share common feelings and be away from the strange routines of the foster family. The irony of the material things around them had been obvious to Jude. She had possessed a black garbage bag with her clothes, two pairs of shoes, and a baggie of toiletries. She struggled to find words to express herself with the parental figures, but the obstacles between her and the biological children in the family had been invisible and impenetrable. "In her imagination," she had often been told.

Her things had been stored in a two-drawer chest from a thrift shop. The fusty odor of someone else's belongings still clung to the interior. When she pulled a sweater over her head, she could smell the fetid recollections of the yarn. The chest wasn't hers, the sweater wasn't hers, nothing was hers.

As Jude walked the beach, she thought maybe she should put her feelings down in words for other foster children. Surely she wasn't the only one who had those feelings of otherness, that desperate need to fit into the unit that she knew would be temporary. *I should be able to release this. I'm an adult now. Others probably struggle with the same inability.*

The walk was longer than normal. Jude got lost in her thoughts and missed the landmark for their turn. Ollie also kept trotting past it, his eyes focused on something down the beach. When they got closer, Jude saw it was a dead fish.

"I bet you'd love to roll on that, but you won't, Mr. Bubba."

Jude tightened the leash and turned to head the opposite direction. Ollie tugged against her, trying to get back to the smelly fish. Jude laughed at him and forced him to follow until he passed her and again began to lead the way.

Jude was struck by how quiet the house was when they entered. She opened the French doors and allowed the cool air inside. Ollie found a spot in the sun and sprawled there for a nap. Jude made a cup of hot tea and took her laptop to the porch. She had just logged on when there was a knock at the front door.

"Hello, I hope I'm not disturbing you. I would've called, but I thought Birdie probably took her phone with her." It was Barry.

"Oh no, you're not disturbing me. Come in." Jude thought it was nice of him to knock. She felt it was actually his house and she was the intruder. "I just got back from a walk on the beach with Ollie." She glanced back at the porch; Ollie was still asleep in the sun. "I must have worn him out. He's snoring out there. Would you like some tea? I just made myself some."

"Sure, that'd be great. I'm not going to make it a habit to drop by. I came to a reunion with some friends of mine, and I thought I'd come by and make sure Birdie got off okay. I called her earlier, but I didn't mention I was staying at a beach house with my friends. I didn't want her to feel like she needed to entertain me or anything while she was getting ready to leave."

"That was thoughtful of you," Jude said. "She was getting a little flustered. Nothing out of the ordinary, just those last-minute jitters. You know, double-checking to make sure she packed everything? When we picked up Maxine and they were talking about the cruise, they were both excited and glowing."

"I'm glad she's doing this. It's good for Birdie to get away, and handy that you're here to take care of Ollie and the house."

Jude handed Barry a mug of tea and led him to the porch. "This has been convenient for me, also, you know. I mean, I thought I would probably return to Austin, but I really didn't have a place to go." Jude told him how she and Birdie met on the beach, explaining the accident and emergency room visit.

"Oh, wow, I didn't realize …. So you really don't have any place to be. You're right. It worked out great for both you and Birdie.

"How does she seem to you? I know you don't really know her that well, but does she seem like she's remembering things and getting along okay? The reason I ask is because of the deal with the pills and my concerns that she seems to be more forgetful. My grandmother, Birdie's mother had dementia."

"I find Birdie delightful," Jude said. "She may be a little forgetful, but it's nothing of consequence. I don't think she's any more forgetful than most people her age. She remembers eventually and laughs at herself. She's cooked some great meals and delights in doing it. We've had some interesting conversations. Birdie has a great sense of humor. People in the neighborhood look out for her, and she has a nice relationship with the owner of the market. He's helpful and more than accommodating. She's also very resourceful. Birdie was instrumental in me getting my belongings back from the car. She contacted a policeman she knows, and he brought it by for me."

"That's good to hear. I guess I don't really have anything to worry about," Barry said.

There was an awkward silence. Barry stared at Ollie, and Jude wondered if she had satisfied his need to stop by and ask about Birdie. She was at a loss about what else to say to him.

"Birdie mentioned some paint in the garage that she bought a while ago to paint the living room and dining room. She said she wanted to brighten it up." Jude fiddled with the handle on the mug, nervous about making conversation with Barry. "I love to paint, and I've been told I'm pretty good. I thought I might surprise her and keep myself busy with a project while she's gone. Do you think that's okay?"

"I can't imagine why not," Barry said. "I'd be willing to pitch in. I'm at loose ends for a while." He smiled and nodded, leading Jude to believe he did think it was a good idea.

"You know the pill incident was a mistake almost anyone could make. The electricity was off, and it was dark. She was embarrassed about it and in hindsight thought she could've used the flashlight, but it hadn't occurred to her at the time. I might've done the same thing," Jude said.

"Yeah, I know. I've realized that. Has Birdie told you anything about her younger years?"

"She's mentioned a good friend named Henry. I sense she didn't feel she belonged. Birdie is what I call a Bohemian," Jude said. She smiled when she thought about why she used the word. "She doesn't march to the same beat as most of the people her age. She might've been ahead of her time in her youth, maybe more liberal than her parents and their friends. I don't know. She wanted to fit, it seems, but she couldn't for some reason."

"According to my father, that's an accurate assessment. My grandparents sent Birdie away when she was in high school.

They always called it a breakdown, but that wasn't fair. It wasn't her. It was them. They wanted her to be reprogramed— the gay prayed out of her," Barry said. His face became unbalanced. He was biting the inside of his cheek. Jude could see he was bothered by what he said.

"I suspected," Jude admitted. "However, I couldn't see that would make much difference to me either way—Birdie's sexuality. But if her parents couldn't accept her the way she was, then I can see why Birdie felt she didn't fit. She couldn't have changed who she was even if she wanted to. I feel for Birdie. I never felt I fit, but my own parents didn't reject me. They just made poor choices for themselves and lost us. Birdie's rejection takes on another layer, docsn't it?"

"Yes, it does. My grandparents were good people. They just weren't educated about … well, about the things we know now. Dad gave me the impression that they thought Birdie was willfully trying to embarrass them or something."

"It was a different time, wasn't it? Did Birdie ever have a relationship or a partner?"

"Yeah, it was a different time. I'm not aware that Aunt Birdie ever had a partner. We've never talked about it. I wouldn't know how to bring that up with her. I wouldn't have talked about a heterosexual relationship either. I guess that's why I feel I'm the only one left who can maybe make it up to her. My parents and grandparents didn't take the time to get to know Birdie. They wanted her to change for them. I think they would've liked her if they had taken the time to try to understand her."

"They would've loved her," Jude corrected. "They missed an opportunity. On the other hand, they created some of her spunk, I think. She can be a little hardheaded, but that's understandable given what you've told me."

Barry laughed. "Yes, she can, hardheaded but softhearted. I would never have made it through losing my own parents if it hadn't been for Aunt Birdie. She was my rock."

"And you were hers, I'm sure."

"Do you have plans for dinner this evening?" Barry asked.

CHAPTER 33

BIRDIE

THE AFTERNOON WAS spent sipping cocktails as the ship drifted away from the dock and headed into the Gulf. Birdie and her friends watched the island fade in the distance, commenting on how different it felt viewing it from the deck of the ship.

They prepared for dinner and the show afterward, putting on their dressy casual outfits to impress the other cruisers.

Seated at a table of four in the main dining room, none of them were disappointed they wouldn't be sharing a table with other travelers. Maxine said she wasn't opposed to it, but she was enjoying having her friends to herself the first night. They raised their glasses of wine in a toast to each other.

Several glasses later, they sat with wistful smiles and after-dinner cordials in front of them. Birdie didn't think she had ever seen the women as relaxed.

Betty's silk blouse had a large pink splotch on the front—a drop of marinara sauce she had rubbed with clumsy hands and an ice cube from her water glass. She finally put the ice down and waved her hand as if to dismiss the issue. She rolled her glassy eyes and pursed her lips. They all giggled.

Birdie wondered if the faces and hands of her friends held the fever of drink that hers did. She hadn't ever consumed the amount of alcohol she did at the dinner. Birdie looked at their faces, leery of their ability to navigate the stairs to the theater. She had doubts that she could keep her head from spinning when she stood.

Maxine was the first to suggest they should leave the table. Birdie took a deep breath and waited until the others were standing before she moved. A sigh of relief escaped her as she thought it would be possible to make an exit without tripping or dragging the tablecloth behind her. It would take dedicated concentration to hold the handrail and take each step down to the theater on the lower deck. She was grateful for the crowd of people heading the same direction; their mass seemed to hide any wobbling and bolster the bodies next to them.

When they were seated in the auditorium, Birdie leaned toward Maxine and whispered, "I'm shitfaced."

"Me, too," Maxine laughed. "We can order another from these waiters in here." She held her hand up and waved to a girl dressed in a red hot pants outfit.

"Are you crazy? No way am I going to have another drink. I'm telling you right now, Maxine, I'll not be responsible for hauling you to our room or sitting up with you if you get sick."

"Oh come on, Birdie. It's our vacation."

"Exactly. I want to enjoy myself, and I certainly don't want to be worried about you falling overboard. Now put your hand down. I'm revoking your license to drink."

Betty and Loretta were peering down the row of seats. "You two okay?" Betty asked.

"We're fine, Sweetie," Maxine said. "Birdie's turned into the house mother and is suggesting I don't have another cocktail."

"I'm with Birdie," Loretta said. "I'm going to pace myself. No sense having all the fun in one day."

"See, Maxine," Birdie hissed. "Control yourself."

Birdie's mood was not enhanced by the alcohol. She didn't enjoy the show, thinking it was amateurish and poorly produced. Her mind wandered. She wanted to be home sitting in her own den with Ollie and Jude. She missed them and knew she would've only had two glasses of wine with dinner. They would've walked on the beach in comfortable clothes, and there would've been no attempts to impress anyone. She chastised herself for being talked into participating in something she abhorred. *Again, I don't fit. I should have known better.*

Maxine, Betty, and Loretta stood and applauded with the rest of the audience, smiling and clapping as if it was the best production they'd ever seen. Birdie stood slowly, glancing at them with raised brows.

"Come on, Birdie. They're young people trying to entertain us. Give them a hand."

Birdie clapped slowly. Loretta motioned to the aisle and urged them to follow her out. When they got to the foyer, she said, "It's best to get out before the cruise director starts talking. That way we can beat the mob trying to get to the stairs and up to the bar. Let's go have a nightcap."

"I'm tired," Birdie said. "I think I'll just go to the room."

"Oh, please, Birdie. Just sit with us for one drink. You can have a decaf. It won't be the same if you're not there."

"All right, just one," Birdie relented, but she wasn't happy about it.

Betty pointed out a cozy booth near the piano and walkway where they could people watch. Birdie was relieved when Maxine ordered coffee also.

"What's wrong, Birdie?" Maxine said. "You look glum."

240

"I think I'm just tired," Birdie lied. "It's been a long day, and more excitement than I'm used to."

Birdie thought it was pleasant to sit and listen to the piano and watch other passengers walking through the bar in their evening clothes. Some people would dance and make requests of the pianist. When they finished their drinks, everyone agreed they were ready to return to their suite.

The cabin had been cleaned and tidied while they were out, and their towels were folded into various animals. They took a few minutes to admire the creativity. "I'm going to put on my pajamas and sit in here before bed," Maxine said.

"I'll join you." Loretta yawned and held her arms in the air to stretch. "It has been a long day, but it's been fun, hasn't it, girls?"

Within thirty minutes they were seated in the living area with the lamps dimmed, and Maxine was pouring cordial glasses of sherry. Birdie accepted the glass, hoping it would help her fall into a restful sleep.

Maybe it was the warm liquid slithering down her throat that loosened Birdie's tongue, for when asked why she had become sullen, she told them she was having flashbacks to high school. "I never fit in," Birdie said. "I'm just fooling myself to think I can enjoy something like this. The whole time we were in that show, I was thinking I wanted to be home with my dog."

"That's called being homesick, Birdie. We all have those feelings. I guarantee you that one out of four people in that theater were probably thinking the same thing," Betty said. "It's hard to be in the moment when we've left something we love behind. Give yourself a day or two. It'll get easier."

"You really think so?" Birdie asked, wondering if what Betty said was true.

"Sure it will," Maxine agreed. "I caught myself thinking about who was at the country club playing bingo. They have a big pot this week, and I'm missing it."

"Hmm, I guess I was just feeling sorry for myself," Birdie said.

"Birdie, I don't know why you always think you're so special and can be the only one who has those feelings. You're not any different than anyone else." Maxine stared at Birdie, sizing her up with her gaze.

"I am different. I know I am. I always have been."

Loretta sat up straighter and leaned forward. "Yes, Birdie, you are different and always have been. You were always the one who refused to follow the crowd. You were the cool one with the black friend, the one who smoked dope on the beach, the one who snuck over to backtrack and stayed until late in the night after we were all in bed. You were the hippie none of us could be because our parents were afraid of long hair and braless girls. You defied convention and rules. You did everything we all wanted to, that we were afraid to do. You had guts, Birdie. We all thought so, and we wanted to be you."

Birdie stared at Loretta and then looked to Maxine, who nodded and gave a crooked grin. "It's true, Birdie. Look at us. We all went by the rules, dressed the way our parents insisted we dress, went through all the motions to keep them pleased, but you, you were the risk taker. The smart girl who wasn't afraid to fail, the girl who rode her bicycle all over town talking to the colorful people, not afraid to show her anger or her joy, wearing clothes you put together from secondhand shops. You were the creative one, the artist, the clever poet, and then something happened. Something none of us were privy to, something that changed you.

"I think I speak for all of us, Birdie," Maxine continued, "It hurt that you couldn't confide in us. I know you must have talked with your friend Harold. That was his name, wasn't it? He must have known your pain, but it hurt that you couldn't confide in us."

"Henry. His name was Henry, and he was my only friend. You all were the friends my parents wanted for me, the daughters of their friends, the good girls. I never was a good girl. I couldn't campaign for cheerleader, homecoming court, student council, any of those popularity deals. I knew I was an outlier. I had no intention of changing my habits to fit what my parents wanted. Henry always warned me our friendship was dangerous." She paused for a beat. "They sent me away, you know? They wanted me to fit in."

"I knew you went off to a boarding school for a while," Loretta said. She took a sip of the sherry and puckered her lips. "I envied that, a chance to go off and be with different people for a spell."

"It wasn't what you think," Birdie said. "It was a program for teenagers who were confused about their sexuality. Our preacher recommended it to my parents. I was supposed to go off and be indoctrinated with new wisdom to make me acceptable and lovable, to make me fit in. All I thought about the whole time I was there was how to exact revenge when I returned." Birdie smirked and squeezed her eyes into little slits. "I stayed awake nights, planning to come back home and fuck every boy in the senior class, just so my parents would beg me not to be heterosexual." She looked around the table. "You girls didn't know I'm a lesbian, did you?"

"Of course we did, Birdie." Maxine grabbed Birdie's hand. "We've loved you regardless. I didn't know that place you went to was supposed to make you straight. That breaks my heart. I've never thought anyone could just change a thing like that. I wanted to ask you about that so many times, but I wasn't sure how you would react. I didn't want to upset you."

"Me, too," Betty said. "I remember when you came back to school. It was a little awkward, but I thought you handled it well. I do recall some rough spots around the season. I mean, it did seem like your mother was at the functions making excuses about why you couldn't attend. Our mothers were tittering about that for a while, but that passed and no one really cared."

"My poor mother," Birdie said. "She wanted me to be a debutant. Part of me begged off to get back at them for the exile and reprogramming attempt, but the other part of me just really didn't want to go through all that hoopla. It would've been torture. I mean really, it would've been more than I could bear."

Birdie took a drink of sherry and thought about the night she missed the ball. "At the same time, I was wrestling with that, my dear friend Henry was in Vietnam. It was such bullshit when you think about it. Nothing made sense, and then there was the racial tension, assassinations and such. Why didn't we think the world was coming to an end? Now we know that war was a lie." Birdie had tears in her eyes as she shook her head.

"You were always so serious about those things, Birdie." Maxine patted Birdie's knee.

"I was. Yes, I felt it to my very core. It was serious stuff, Maxine," Birdie huffed. She glanced at Maxine and moved her hand. She squinted her eyes, then closed them, shaking her head again. "I wanted to march with those protesters and run off to Canada with Henry and never come back. I had this passion burning in my chest to fight all the things that were wrong, including my parents trying to change who I was, who I am.

"I should've known you girls knew about me. I was afraid to bring it up, too. I didn't know how to say it, and I never saw a reason to actually *come out* after the years went by."

"This can be your coming out." Loretta held the cordial glass in the air. "I would like to propose a toast to the coolest girl in high school, the girl with an independent streak attempting to mask her sexuality. We lived through it and are here to see a new day and celebrate being ourselves. To Birdie and the Cruisers."

"To Birdie and the Cruisers," they said in unison.

Birdie's eyes glistened as she stared at the faces of the women she had known as girls. What a relief it would've been to be able to share a beer with them on the beach, sitting in a circle barefoot with Henry. Why couldn't that have happened? What made them think it could happen? They still didn't get it, and they never would.

CHAPTER 34

JUDE

BARRY HAD ANOTHER two days at the beach house rental on the west end of the island. He invited Jude to join him for grilled steaks and suggested they take Ollie. Jude accepted, grabbing a bottle of wine and her sweater.

They stopped at the market, Jude and Ollie sitting in the car while Barry shopped for the steaks and makings for a salad and potatoes. Jude watched shoppers walk across the parking lot and enter the store. She was pain-free and feeling relaxed. Her quiet stay at Birdie's had turned into more social life than she had enjoyed in a long while.

Before Barry started the grill, they walked the beach with Ollie running ahead of them, charging a flock of seagulls standing on the water's edge. Jude had not been beyond the seawall and enjoyed being able to walk directly from the house to the water. The beach was much less populated; in fact, they were the only people there.

The rental was built on stilts, with parking on the ground level under the structure. At one end there was a patio with lounge chairs, a fire pit, and a hammock. Up long wooden stairs sat a wide deck facing the Gulf with a wall of windows and sliding doors on the back of the house.

When they returned from their walk, Ollie curled up next to the fire pit and Barry started the grill. Jude helped prepare the salad while Barry put the potatoes in the oven and rubbed the steaks with seasonings.

The sun was setting, and Jude put her sweater over her shoulders as they sat facing the Gulf with glasses of wine while the steaks cooked. Jude thought about how comfortable she felt just sitting, feeling no need to fill the silence. It was nice being able to be on the beach. She knew she was in the moment, and she was afraid she wouldn't have many more like the one she was experiencing.

"I have a confession to make," Barry said. "I actually took some vacation time to be here for these days Birdie is gone, because I thought she'd need me to house-sit when she told me about the cruise. Then when she told me I wasn't needed, I just took the days anyway and rented this house so some buddies could come hang out for a while. I was a little disappointed that

Birdie didn't need me. I don't know why I argued with her about not telling me about the cruise. She did in a roundabout way, but she was vague about the dates. We just tend to get into these squabbles sometimes. They're about nothing."

Jude smiled. "Miscommunication, or no communication. I'm sorry that happened. I know what you mean. I can see how a person might tend to be oppositional with Birdie. She's in control most of the time. Has it been an inconvenience?"

"Not really, I guess. I'm not one to take a change of plans in stride, but I got over it. They were my plans and not Birdie's."

Jude stared at Barry, pursing her lips. "I'm having trouble mustering any sympathy for your situation. My plans have been derailed big-time. I've lost my best friend, my apartment, the trip we planned together. It's still hard for me to accept what's happened the last few weeks."

"I'm sorry. I shouldn't be whining about Birdie. I didn't mean … I wasn't thinking. Of course this inconvenience is nothing compared to what you've gone through."

"No, I know that wasn't your intention. I just meant I know how it feels to have your plans altered. I'm pretty flexible. I guess that comes from moving to so many different homes when I was younger. In college I got used to the routine and being my own decision-maker. I really liked that, and all of a sudden here I am, living in someone else's home again and feeling a little out of control. I have no complaints, of course. It's just very different than I had planned."

"I have no idea what that's like," Barry said. "My life has been very sheltered compared to yours."

Jude enjoyed talking with Barry. They discussed everything, and she felt comfortable telling him things she had not shared with anyone else. She had no filter and said what she was thinking to him. The meal was delicious, and she helped him wash the dishes.

"I should've driven Birdie's car down here so you wouldn't have to drive me back to town." Jude said, as a hint she was ready to leave. She didn't want to get too comfortable at the beach house.

"I don't mind. I like to ride on the seawall in the evening."

There was an innocence about Barry. He was easygoing and comfortable. She couldn't understand why Birdie would get so irritated with him, though she supposed it was his concern for her health and his hovering. Jude could see how Birdie would feel that he was trying to usurp her independence.

As Barry drove them back to Birdie's, Ollie stood in the back seat, his head out the window with his nose toward the water. Jude laughed when she turned to glance at him, the wind blowing his fur wildly around his face.

"Thanks for that outing, Barry," Jude said as they pulled up in front of Birdie's. "It was nice to get out and see another part of the island. I know Ollie enjoyed the romp on the beach and that ride home."

Jude opened the door and put Ollie's leash on him to lead him up to the house.

"No need to get out, Barry. We can manage. Thank you again."

"Sure, let me know if you need anything."

Jude closed the door and turned to wave. She wasn't sure what type of goodbye she should give Barry, but she wanted to keep him in the car and not on the porch. It was just too much to think about. He was nice and attractive, but Jude wasn't looking for a relationship. She was almost certain she was facing a major health crisis.

She contemplated renting a small efficiency apartment closer to the university when Birdie returned, possibly a place close enough to walk to the healthcare she might need. She had been looking at the real estate ads.

The only problem with that idea was that Birdie might feel some obligation to her. Jude didn't want that. She didn't want to be a burden to anyone. She just wanted to help Birdie find her authentic self and then leave peacefully. It was something that hadn't occurred to her before, but she knew it was what she was meant to do.

When they entered the house, Jude stubbed her toe on Casey's backpack. It didn't budge. She tried to pick it up, but she couldn't lift it. *What in the world could make it that heavy?*

Jude sat down on the floor and tugged at the zippers, opening all the compartments of the backpack. It was stuffed. She took out the contents, stacking them in piles on the floor next to her, just inside the dining room. When everything was out, Jude again tried to lift the bag. It was still heavy, but not immovable. She ran her hand against the lining. There was something there.

Jude got the kitchen shears and began cutting through the lining. There were bundles of large bills sewn into the interior lining of the backpack. Jude worked until she'd removed all the money. "Holy shit! Maybe this is why Jax was so intent on getting to Casey. *She must have robbed his stash.*" He was *definitely a drug dealer*.

Jude repacked the backpack with Casey's belongings and got a plastic grocery bag for the money. She wanted to count it, but she was feeling light headed. She put all of Casey's identification in the bag with the money. Before going upstairs, Jude verified Ollie was on his pillow in the living room. She placed the bag in the empty bottom drawer of the chest in the guest room.

Shooting pains began to plague Jude after she had showered to get ready for bed. They caused her to curl up in response to the spasms that radiated to her back. She fumbled her way to the bathroom to take the pills she had been given in the ER.

Sliding to the floor in the bathroom, Jude sat with her forehead on her knees on the cool tile. She leaned back on the tub and slumped against the wall. *I'll just sit here until this pain subsides.*

It was 4:00 a.m. when Jude made her way back to the bed. She wanted to be able to start the painting the following day, but if the pain didn't subside, there was no way she could manage the project. She tilted her head back on the pillow and closed her eyes tightly, willing the pain to go away and allow her to do the things she wanted to accomplish while Birdie was gone.

Pain and exhaustion had Jude so distracted she couldn't even think about the large amount of cash she found in Casey's backpack.

CHAPTER 35

BIRDIE

THEY SLEPT LATE the following morning, the first full day of cruising. Birdie's head throbbed as she rolled over in bed to face the parted drapery. Bright shards of sunlight shot into the room, making her wince. She could hear Maxine's wheezy snore and knew she wouldn't be falling back to sleep. She needed water. Her throat was dry and scratchy.

Fumbling for her robe, Birdie felt her way along the desk opposite their beds. The contrast of dark and light played tricks on her eyes. She went into the common area to use the half bath without waking anyone else. She poured a glass of water from a bottle in the mini fridge and took an aspirin from her purse. Grabbing her sunglasses, she went outside to sit on the balcony.

The humidity hit her in the face when she eased the sliding door open. Her eyes watered, sending tears down her cheeks.

I'll have to wear a hat all day or wash my hair. Why did I have all those drinks? This throbbing in my temples has to be temporary.

There was nothing to look at but water, choppy waves for as far as the eye could see. Birdie lifted her sunglasses, but she immediately replaced them, cringing at the bright reflection, her head tight and achy.

The door slid open, and Birdie turned to see Betty stepping out onto the balcony. "I vote we sit on the deck in our bathing suits and play mah-jongg all day. I have no energy for anything else. How did we get so old?"

"Speak for yourself," Birdie laughed. "I went to kindergarten, so I got to skip a grade. You girls are a whole year older than me, which means you should know better."

"You're right. We always have been a bad influence for each other. Loretta was right last night when she said we idolized you, Birdie. We always wanted to be as brave as you were. I didn't have the nerve to break rank and do anything different. You, on the other hand, were courageous and willful."

"I didn't feel courageous. I always felt like a fraud. The only time I felt like myself was when I was with Henry."

"I wish I'd had a Henry, someone to understand what I was feeling. You know us girls just always said what we thought the other wanted to hear. We didn't ever tell the truth, did we?"

"Never, bunch of lying bitches," Birdie giggled.

"Takes one to know one. Now, they have these marvelous waffles on the buffet that are about an inch thick. The syrup and butter pool in those little squares. You can pile them with berries and have a big tall glass of orange juice. I think it would make me feel so much better if I could feel that syrup on my tongue."

"Oh for heaven's sake, Betty. You make it sound like a religious experience."

"I believe it could be. You want to try it? We could go to confession after. 'Bless me, Father, for I have partaken of the crispiest waffle on the sea.'"

When Birdie and Betty reentered the suite, Loretta and Maxine were stirring. Maxine had on her suit and cover-up. "I'm not putting on a speck of makeup until this evening," she said. "I can't stand to think about it. My face hurts."

"I'm with you, sister. I just talked Birdie into visiting the buffet with me. How about you?"

"Sure. I want carbs and sugar for some reason."

Birdie laughed. "I guess we're all of the same notion on that. Betty just described a waffle like it was some kind of work of art, and now I can't think of anything else."

Loretta joined them and they left the suite with their large sun hats, caftans, and sunglasses over swollen eyes. They moved slowly down the corridor. Betty held her arms out, bouncing off the walls as if they were bumper pads as she swayed with the motion of the ship. Maxine had the mah-jongg set slung over her shoulder.

Birdie was relieved when the elevator door opened and there was no one there. She didn't like the awkward silence or mindless chitchat on the elevator. She just wanted to scream, "Bullshit!" and get off when an older guy in a Hawaiian shirt chatted them up.

They went up two floors to the pool deck and crossed in front of people already sprawled on lounge chairs in the sun.

Maxine pointed to a table for four close to the glass wall and near the restaurant door, "Let's put our stuff down here. We can eat some breakfast here and then play the game." They all nodded in agreement.

Birdie felt her eyes grow heavy. She thought she might need a nap before they tackled another evening. Part of her thought it must be relaxation, but the other part of her felt she had been drugged.

Betty was right about the waffles. They were heaven, and Birdie sprinkled powdered sugar on them as well. Her first sip of hot coffee made her eyes roll back in her head. "This is just decadent, isn't it? Not just the food and this wonderful coffee, but the view and the thought of not having to do anything if we don't want to. It's just wonderful. I think I'm getting the hang of it. Can I get a hallelujah?"

Maxine shook her bright orange fingernail in Birdie's direction. "I'm not going to tell you I told you so, but I told you so."

Birdie grinned, "Yes, you did."

They spent the morning playing mah-jongg and taking dips in the hot tubs. They took short breaks to sit and people watch.

"There's that couple again," Loretta said. "Over to the left. She's a lot older than him, don't you think? Look at that scar on her thighs. Do you think that's liposuction? His skin isn't sagging anywhere. There's a story there, I guarantee it."

Maxine looked over her glasses in the couple's direction. "They aren't as interesting to me as the blonde over there across the deck with those two old geezers. What do you think the story is there? Could be a daughter with her uncle and father?"

"That's your assignment, Mac. You strike up a conversation with them and report back. You have twenty-four hours," Betty said.

"I'll see what I can do." Maxine winked at Betty.

They wandered into the solarium to eat a light lunch. There was soft music playing, and most of the people were sitting in lounge chairs reading or sleeping with their mouths hanging open. "Girls, if you see me snoring on the deck chair, wake me up and roll me over," Loretta said. "Better yet, hold a pillow over my face."

"Will do, and I expect the same courtesy," Maxine laughed.

Birdie got a kick out of listening to her friends' banter. She suspected they were much the same as they had been growing up. It was possible that she was the subject of many of their conversations and speculations. She wondered if they often challenged Maxine to investigate her and get back to them with information. If her parents considered her an oddity, certainly their friends did also.

She wiped her mouth with a napkin and took a sip of iced tea, conscious of the fact that she had grown quiet and her mood was changing. Minutes earlier she was enjoying herself, but now their easy chats with each other made Birdie aware she was not a part of their prattle. She didn't know why it dampened her mood, because she really didn't want to be an accomplice in the gossip. *She thought it was rude. Can others tell they're gossiping?*

This was the part of their little group that Birdie didn't like. There was a judgment about others that occurred every time they were together. It wasn't attractive or flattering to the women, and she didn't want to be a part of it, but she also didn't want to scold them.

She only wanted to walk off and find Henry. The two of them could find a quiet place on a lower deck to smoke a joint and watch the water. He would've liked the ship. They used to sit behind the parked trains, gazing at the ships and imagining their innards. Henry would make up stories about the decks, ladders, and bunk beds inside the ships parked in the harbor. He would've been designing the interiors, not berating the crew.

CHAPTER 36

JUDE & BARRY

PANCREAS, THEY TOLD her. Jude sat in one of the small cubicles of the emergency room. She had driven herself there after she fed Ollie and let him out. The pills she had been given after the accident weren't effective anymore.

"You understand there's no recommended treatment unless you want to go to MD Anderson and see if they might be doing a medication trial. I can make the referral." A tall woman with dark hair was looking at her with drooping eyes. She had taken her glasses off and wiped at the edge of her eyebrow. Jude stared back at her, wondering if these sad eyes were for her condition or if the doctor always had such sloping lids.

The sight of the doctor and the aroma of alcohol and maybe urine made Jude squeeze her eyes shut. It blocked the sight but not the odor. She sighed and opened her eyes. Dr. Raschid was still there.

"I know," Jude responded. "And no, I don't have the money or means to go to Houston. I'm aware it's not a good prognosis. I only thought maybe the pain could be managed. I sat on the bathroom floor all night. It was miserable. I guess I'm just feeling sorry for myself, wishing I could not be so aware of it."

"I'm sorry, Ms. Reynolds. I know this is difficult. Is there someone here with you, anyone you might call?"

"No, there's no one. I don't have anyone."

"Would you like to meet with the social worker?"

"No, no thank you. I've had enough social workers to last me until next week, or my lifetime, whichever comes first." Jude was aware she was being sarcastic. Dr. Droopy Eyes didn't deserve that, but Jude was feeling a little hopeless; maybe the dark humor could improve her mood.

"So, I'll just put on my clothes and be on my way," Jude said. "You wouldn't have any herbal recommendation or tea concoctions that might help with the pain?"

"Those pills you were prescribed are the highest dose we can do safely. I can refer you to pain management."

"Can I call you about that? I don't want to have to come to the ER every time there's an issue."

"Sure. You'll need to pay the desk before you leave and we'll …. Just do that, and I'll take care of everything else."

Jude left the emergency room and drove down the seawall toward Birdie's street. She pulled over, then did a U-turn to face east. The sun was glistening on the water, the pain a distant thrum deep inside her. She put her head back and let her eyes focus on a distant gull. Joggers and people on bicycles sped by, but Jude maintained her gaze, daring the ache to return.

Tears welled in her eyes and for the first time, she thought it wasn't fair. She was in her twenties, too young for such violence in her body. There was the money she found in Casey's backpack, and even though it looked like it could be tens of thousands, Jude was sure it wasn't enough for cancer treatment that might not work.

For over an hour, Jude argued with herself, wondered about her biological family's medical history, swore off diet soft drinks, and tried to bargain with whoever was in charge. That bargaining had never worked out before. In fact, it might be why she didn't even consider praying. Dr. Droopy Eyes had offered a social worker, but not a speck of hope.

Jude glanced down at her phone. There was a text message from Birdie: *In Key West. Having a great time. See you next week.*

She smiled. Birdie had complained about texting, but agreed to do it when they were in port, and it wouldn't cost so much. Jude texted back, *All is well. Ollie is fine. Have fun.*

Part of Jude's text was true. She would have to decide how to manage a departure when Birdie returned. Where would she go? How would she manage her medical needs? Those were things she needed to decide before Birdie came home.

Jude sat up behind the wheel and decided to go home and take Ollie for a walk on the beach. Maybe the sand and salt air could clear her head.

When Jude turned down Birdie's street, she saw Barry's car in front of the house. He was standing on the back porch as she pulled toward the garage off the alley. She took a deep breath, steeling herself to face him.

"Hey, Barry," Jude said as she closed the car door.

"Hey. Uh, you don't look so good. You okay?"

Jude decided to be honest. "I went to the ER. It's a pain in my stomach I can't get rid of. Not much help there, three hundred dollars later."

"You don't think you had food poisoning, do you? I didn't notice anything."

"Oh no, nothing like that. This is a chronic thing I've been dealing with. It'll pass, I'm sure. I was going to take Ollie for a walk."

"Are you sure you're up to that? You look exhausted. I can take him while you get a nap."

"Oh, well, that would be nice. I didn't get any sleep last night. I thought maybe a walk on the beach might make me feel better, but you're probably right, sleep should be the priority."

"I'm at loose ends today. I was going to see if you wanted to go to lunch on the harbor, but I'll do the walk with Ollie and you go up and get some sleep. I'll wait around for you to wake up. I have a good book in the car."

"Okay, that sounds good. Thanks, Barry."

"No problem."

Jude pointed out the paint to Barry as they walked through the garage. She put her purse and the papers from her ER visit on the kitchen table, then went to the sink and got water to take two pills, hoping they would help her sleep.

Barry shouted goodbye from the front porch, and Jude made her way upstairs. She sat on the side of the bed and slipped her shoes off, aware of her fatigue. There was something she wanted to do before she forgot.

Taking a piece of paper from a tablet in her backpack, Jude wrote a note and placed it inside the plastic bag with the money in the bottom drawer of the chest beside the bed. It was addressed to Birdie or Barry, or whoever found the bag. The note said: *Use this money as you see fit. Start a scholarship, donate it to the charity of your choice, or take a vacation. It's for the pure enjoyment of those people who made my last few days on earth bearable. Thank you! Jude.*

Easing under a throw, Jude relaxed into the bed and drifted off to sleep.

Ollie pulled Barry to walk east, but Barry insisted they go west toward 25th Street. After tugging toward the more familiar route, Ollie sighed and gave up, trotting ahead of Barry into more congested foot traffic. There were more feet, more smells and fewer opportunities to stand at the edge of the wall and sniff the water. It wasn't Ollie's idea of a relaxing stroll, and there were fewer birds to harass. His only hope was that Barry knew where the treats were kept when they returned to Birdie's.

Barry was familiar with the treat jar and offered Ollie one when he had detached the leash. He also felt hungry, so he opened the refrigerator to look for a snack. Pushing the milk container aside, he spotted the plastic container of soup and heated a portion in the microwave, recognizing Birdie's chicken soup concoction. It was one of his favorites.

Finished, he cleaned up the dishes he'd used. When he was putting them away, he noticed the pills Jude left beside the kitchen sink. Reading the label, he was surprised they were for pain.

The newspaper was still rolled in plastic on the kitchen table. Barry eyed Jude's purse and the papers next to it. He unrolled the newspaper and sat in Birdie's chair, turning on the television to the smooth jazz station. He read through the paper, noting two people in the obituaries, the parents of girls he knew in high school. Putting the newspaper aside and sliding lower in the chair, Barry rested his head and put his feet on the ottoman.

Two hours later, Barry startled awake, aware his mouth was open, and he had a crick in his neck. He glanced at his watch, surprised he had slept so long. Rubbing his face, he moved to stand and head to the kitchen to make himself a cup of coffee. The reason he came to the house was to see Jude. Maybe if he stalled longer, she would wake and feel better, good enough to join him for dinner on the harbor.

While the coffee was brewing, Barry tidied the table, collecting the plastic from the newspaper. He glanced at the papers next to Jude's purse. Something caught his eye: "Stage IV."

Barry picked up the papers and read the contents. "Refused referral to MD Anderson, refused referral to social worker, accepted follow-up for pain management." These notes were scribbled after the release diagnosis. It was also noted that Jude weighed five pounds less than the previous visit.

There was a bead of sweat forming on Barry's upper lip. He fumbled with the papers, trying to replace them next to Jude's purse exactly as they had been. The coffee pot sputtered, as it would do when the brewing cycle was complete. Barry poured himself a mug and took it to the back porch where Ollie was asleep in a sunny spot on the rug.

He sipped coffee, trying to come to grips with Jude's diagnosis. It wasn't long before Barry heard movement in the kitchen and Jude appeared with her own mug of coffee. "The aroma pulled me out of my nap," Jude said.

"Sorry, I fell asleep, too, and thought it might perk me up."

"No worries. I'm rested and ready to join the living."

Barry was quiet. Jude thought he seemed weird, not his normal, relaxed self. She allowed the lull, not feeling a need to fill the space with chat.

"You slept?" Barry asked.

"Yes, I didn't sleep at all last night. That's why I went in to the ER. I can't have many more nights like that."

"You've lost weight since the first time I saw you. I can see it in your face."

"Hmm, not that I've noticed. Maybe a few pounds. I don't see how, though, with Birdie's great cooking and that meal I had at the beach house last night."

"You're sick, aren't you, Jude?" Barry said.

"I've been having a deal with my stomach. Yes, just what I told you."

"No, I mean you've got something that can't be cured, like cancer."

Jude didn't feel like trying to evade the issue. It took too much energy to concoct a story. "Yes, it's pancreatic. The symptoms started a few months ago, but I didn't think it was anything. Then when I was taken to the emergency room by ambulance after the accident, my bloodwork was a mess, so they continued to probe and test. That's when I learned it was inoperable and terminal. They showed me all the scans and pictures.

"When I left the ER, I felt pretty hopeless, and I was afraid Casey's boyfriend was still looking for us. I walked straight toward the sound of the waves. Birdie found me there. Until I saw her face, I fully intended to be there on the beach until I stopped breathing."

"She nursed you and gave you shelter from the storm." Barry smiled.

"She did, but then she gave me something else, something I wasn't ready to give up on. She accepted me." Jude shrugged and pursed her lips, her eyes full of tears. "I wasn't ready for that. I had just convinced myself to die by the ocean."

"You're too young to die, Jude. Surely there's some treatment, something you can try. The best cancer hospital in the country is right down the road."

"I know, but the doctor was honest. I've seen two now, and they were both painfully honest. There might be an experimental treatment, and it might prolong my life, but I don't think the quality of life would be much. I've read up on it. I've looked at the trials online and emailed the clinics. They don't offer much encouragement."

"I'm sorry. Sorry for you, and I'm sorry for Birdie. Does she know?" Barry asked.

"No, I haven't told her. I was just thinking about that this morning. I think I should make arrangements to go back to Austin, maybe get a little apartment near the hospital or something. I was thinking about an efficiency here, but I don't want to be a burden. I think it would be better if I leave when Birdie comes back. You know, my job here is done and I'm moving on."

"Well, I'm sorry for Birdie, but I'm sorry for me, too. I wanted to get to know you better." Barry stared at the floor. "You know, it's not fair to Birdie for you to just leave and not tell her. She thinks of you as more than a house sitter, you know?"

"I know."

"You don't have anyone to help you with this, Jude. Stay here. We'll help you."

"That's nice of you to offer, Barry, but this is not your house. It's Birdie's. I've already said I don't want the burden of my illness on anyone else. That would make me feel terrible. I don't want to talk about this anymore. My stomach is feeling much better and I want to enjoy the times when I'm feeling halfway decent."

"I understand. I'll drop it for now, but I think we need to talk about it again. Don't dwell on it, but don't shut me out. Can we go out for dinner?"

CHAPTER 37

BIRDIE

MAXINE LED THE way down the long dock back to the ship. She turned, looking back at the other three as she tried to hurry them to the gangplank. "We're the last ones to get back. Look, there's smoke coming out of the stack. They're cranking up to pull away. The captain will be saying our names over the loudspeaker, asking if anyone saw us being hauled off to jail."

Birdie giggled, along with Loretta and Betty. They had fun, but nothing to be arrested for. Betty was laden with bags of souvenirs for her grandchildren. Loretta offered to carry a couple to hurry her along.

"These are heavy," she complained.

"Ten T-shirts weigh a lot," Betty said.

The crew teased them as they slid their cards through the reentry scanner. "You're the last cruisers to return, ladies. We always take bets on who it will be. None of you were on the list." He winked at Birdie.

"They're a bad influence," Birdie said. "I want you to know that I refused to have anything to do with them until recently."

"Nonsense," Maxine called out. "She's the ringleader." Maxine hurried down the corridor, having already announced that she had to go to the bathroom. The others giggled, watching her from behind, wondering why she refused to visit the ladies' room in Sloppy Joe's as they had.

Birdie plopped on the sofa in the living area of the suite. Her feet ached, and she was tired. She had an uneasy feeling. Jude's text back to her earlier in the day was short and said Ollie was fine, but she was more worried about Jude. She had been having those pains, and Birdie feared it was more than just a bug.

"What's wrong, Birdie?" Maxine asked. "You look like you lost your best friend."

"I was just thinking about Jude. She wasn't feeling well the day before we left. I'm worried that she might be sick."

"The house sitter?"

"Well yes, she agreed to care for Ollie and stay at the house, but she's also my friend. I feel responsible for her and ... oh, never mind."

"Come on, say what you meant to say. If it's troubling you, get it out."

"Well, Jude reminds me of Henry. We have that kind of friendship. I don't want anything to happen to her. She's special."

"Oh, sweetie, I understand. I do, but you worry too much. Didn't you have a good time today?" Maxine said.

"It was wonderful. I had a great time. Key West is a lovely place, so diverse. I didn't realize it had so many Victorian houses. It reminds me of home in a way, the artists, the quaint eateries, the casual, laid-back atmosphere. It was all wonderful."

Birdie's hunch bothered her. She put on a pleasant face over dinner, but in the back of her mind, she was hoping Jude would know where to ask for help if she needed it. She regretted that she had been so distant with Barry over the last few weeks.

Stay in the now, stop fretting over something that may not even be.

The productions in the theater were improving, Birdie thought. They attended nightly, sitting close to the back so they could exit quickly. They always went to the piano bar and tried to snag the same booth.

Birdie was convinced she could've had these women as her best friends when she was younger. She had been the one to keep them at a distance. They were willing and accepted her.

She thought they really did think she was cool back in the day. She felt bad for misjudging.

However, Birdie told herself, if she had embraced this crew, she would not have had Henry. He wouldn't have been able to have the long talks with her on the beach, or the sardines in the float warehouses. Those cherished memories would've been impossible. Birdie would probably have been attending all the parties of the season, not even thinking about where Henry was and what he was doing. No, she wouldn't have changed that.

When they were back in the suite, seated around the coffee table in their pajamas, Maxine said, "Birdie, tell me what was so special about Henry. Why him? Of all the people you could've adopted, why him?"

"I didn't adopt him, Maxine. It wasn't like that. We found each other, or he found me. We had a mutual respect for each other. I remember the first day we talked. I had seen him at school, a little shy, tall for his age, and always smiling."

Birdie proceeded to tell them what drew her to Henry. He spotted her crying under the stairs as there were masses of students in the hall changing classes. He reversed his direction and went back to check on her. She didn't tell him that day why she was crying—it was a couple of years later before she admitted it to him—but he told her a story about himself, an embarrassment he had, and it made Birdie giggle.

"He took the time to come back to me and try to change my day with his words. No one had ever done that for me before. Even my family thought my feelings weren't true. They wanted me to be different, but they never cared where the feelings came from." Birdie unscrewed the cap on a bottle of water and took a sip. She rubbed the ridges on the cap with her painted fingernail. "The feelings I had could never just be mine. I always had to be the one to change. Henry knew that. I couldn't change my sexuality, and he couldn't change his color. We never said that, but we both knew it. No one, and I mean no one could ever do what Henry did for me. I loved him.

"Our souls knew each other. There were times, when we sat on the beach, that both of us knew we had been there before."

"What do you mean, been there?" Betty asked. She had tears in her eyes. They were all listening to Birdie, touched by her intense feeling for Henry.

"We thought we had known each other in another place in another life, but in this world. We recognized each other. I don't know how to describe it. We saw each other, but it wasn't our faces, or our bodies. It was our spirit, our very being, the way we were in the world. We had come from another place together to be reconnected on the beach."

"My brother said you and Henry smoked pot down there on the beach," Loretta said. "Maybe that's what it was. You were hallucinating." The other women giggled.

"We did smoke pot. We drank beer, too. Your brother would know, Loretta, because he bought it for us. He spoke very rudely to Henry, by the way. He took a condescending tone that didn't sit well with me, but he didn't mind taking our money to make a profit." Birdie's eyes watered, and her lips drew in a tight line. The mention of Loretta's brother reminded Birdie of one of the worst days of her life. Her eyes flashed at Loretta. "You can relay that to him next Thanksgiving when you're all around the table. Ask him about his drug-dealing days. That's the only reason he would've had to have a conversation with me. I wish you could've asked him in front of your father, the district attorney when we were in high school. I'm sure he'd like to hear a good story about the good old days." Birdie was irritated with Loretta's comment, and she didn't mind letting her know. Maxine squirmed at Birdie's response, but Birdie didn't care.

"I know people wagged their tongues and expected me to come up pregnant with a black baby. Surely that's why my parents were so anxious to get me out of town. They wouldn't believe my pleas and assurances that I wouldn't have sex with a boy because I would prefer a girl. That really threw them for a loop.

"Here's what really plucked my nerves: the holier-than-thou white guys who were so eager to talk about something they knew nothing about. Your brother, the football hero, college boy, was one of them, Loretta. I can barely be civil to him, even now." Birdie stood, her hands shaking with anger.

"I've said my piece about my relationship with Henry. I'm remembering things I don't want to remember, and now I'm going to say good night."

Birdie went to the bedroom and crawled in the bed that had been turned down while they were at dinner. She moved the wrapped chocolate to the nightstand, staring at the foil wrapper like it was betrayal.

She wouldn't be able to fall asleep. Loretta had sparked a memory, a painful situation she wanted to erase. She knew what Henry had told her, but she suspected there was more to the story. Something that would bring it right back to her. She had felt responsible at the time, but Henry assured her it wasn't her fault. "If it hadn't been you, it would've been something else, Birdie," Henry had said.

She could still see him standing in front of her. She looked at him through pools of liquid in her eyes, his body wavy through the tears. She would blink, the tears would flush from her eyes, and Henry would be gone.

CHAPTER 38

JUDE

JUDE WENT UPSTAIRS to wash her face and comb her hair. She didn't really want to go out, but she didn't want Barry to leave either. She was afraid to be alone, afraid the pain would come back, and she knew there was nothing to be done. The medicine she had was the only salve, and it didn't work.

They sat on the deck of Barry's favorite restaurant on the harbor. Jude ordered soup. The sunset was impressive, and there were dolphins jumping in front of the large barges. Barry drank a glass of wine. It was nice to share a meal and sit by the water.

"You know, I haven't had many days like this. My whole life, I wouldn't have had an opportunity to eat at a place like this or sit outside by the water and watch the sunset. It's ironic that it happens now."

The sun was down and it was dark. The torches around the deck were flickering and casting reflections on the water. They watched people walk on the docks and ride bicycles toward Harborside. Jude would not have thought she would've experienced such an evening in south Texas. She had been anticipating quaint restaurants in Europe with Casey. She was thinking about how one day had changed everything.

"I would've thought you might've had the opportunity in Austin, out by the lake. There are plenty of scenic places for a meal there. I'm thinking it's ironic, too, that I should meet you just as you're leaving." Barry said.

"You're right about the places around the lake. We just never took advantage of such a thing, Casey and I. We worked, studied, went to 6th Street on our off time, and that was it. I was limited by transportation. I just had my trusty bicycle unless Casey was off. I don't know what to think about all this. I can't make much sense of it," Jude said.

"I think when you can't make sense of it, it's not supposed to make sense. Can you imagine what Birdie would think if she were here, you and I having dinner together being all philosophical?" Barry said.

He looked at Jude with kind eyes, but they seemed a little sad. The waiter took his plate and poured more water. They were quiet, not wanting anyone else to hear their conversation.

Jude had no more words to say. She thought she had said everything.

"I don't really have to explain anything to you, do I? I mean, you understand it's probably just a matter of weeks." She put her hand to her mouth and pressed her finger against her upper lip. There wasn't much light on the deck, and she felt safe there even if she shed some tears. "I'm scared, Barry. I'm scared of the things I don't know, and the night scares me the most. I didn't know this would happen this fast. I shouldn't have agreed to stay."

"You were trying to help Birdie." Barry glanced around like he was searching for words, then let out a long sigh. "I have an idea. You can say no, and I'll understand. I'm off for a while. The lease on the beach house is up in two days. I can be with you. I can come back to Birdie's and stay after the lease is up until she returns. You don't have to be scared or alone."

"That's nice, but I don't want to inconvenience you."

"I want to, Jude, I really want to. I wouldn't feel comfortable leaving you there alone. I have another idea, and I think it'll help, but I can't tell you until we get back to Birdie's." He smiled and raised his eyebrows. "I'm pretty sure it's just what the doctor would order if she could."

Jude smiled and tilted her head. "Well, I like surprises, and that sounds intriguing. I'll just have to wait, I suppose."

Jude had eaten very little of the soup. It had grown cold and the waiter took it away. Barry paid the bill. They walked the short distance to the dock to watch the lights on the water and then returned to Birdie's.

Barry went straight to the kitchen and was rummaging around in the freezer. "Aha," he said. "Birdie's so predictable." He pulled out a brown paper bag, stuck his hand inside, and pulled out what looked like chocolate cake wrapped in plastic. "Birdie's classic brownies."

"Oh, that's nice, Barry, but I really don't feel like anything else to eat," Jude said, waving her hand and turning up her nose.

"I think you might like these brownies. They're magic."

Jude smiled, and then her eyes widened. "Oh, you mean like in medicinal marijuana?"

"Exactly." Barry grinned and took a couple of brownies from the bag, replacing the rest in the freezer. He continued to rummage in the freezer. "Yep, right where it's always been. Look at this." Barry pulled out a cardboard popsicle box. When he dumped out the contents, it was a plastic bag of marijuana and rolling papers.

"No way," Jude said. "Birdie is a dope fiend."

"Yep, the oldest hippie I know. But seriously, Jude, this could be just what you need to fight those pains."

"Well, I hate to pilfer Birdie's stash, but I'll try just about anything."

"So, why don't you go gather some things and come back to the beach house with me? We'll take Ollie and stay until the lease is up, and then we'll come back here. I'm not asking you to sleep with me or anything—unless you want to, of course—but we'll have this wonderful medicine and you won't be alone."

Jude had tears in her eyes. She moved toward him and put her forehead on his shoulder. They stood in Birdie's kitchen with their arms around each other. "That's what I need, just someone to be with me and something for the pain. That's all I need, I think."

"You go get your things. I'll get Ollie's food and bowls and pack this magic dust."

Jude took her time ascending the stairs. She wondered if she should return to the kitchen and tell Barry she didn't want to go to the beach house. She should stay in Birdie's house, alone, and think. Maybe she should ponder her circumstances and come to some appropriate decision about her limited future.

She sat on the unmade bed in the guest room. *What's happening?*

CHAPTER 39

BIRDIE

AT BREAKFAST THERE was a change in mood. Birdie moved around the buffet, distracted by inconsiderate people who allowed the spoon to sink into the sausage gravy with no attempt to retrieve it for the next in line. She clucked her tongue, irritated by people she didn't know.

Her conversation with Loretta the previous evening was crawling over her. It reminded her of a dark time, a time when she and Henry almost ran away. It was a time when nothing could convince her that anyone but Henry could possibly have her best interest at heart.

Birdie's brother, Pete, was on the football team. An upperclassman, he was vaguely aware that his sister left on her bicycle and was gone from home most of the day. She was younger; he was admired by other players and the girls. Pete was unconcerned about his socially awkward kid sister, Birdie. Then he began to hear rumors about a boy, one from the housing projects. He followed Birdie one day and saw her with Henry on the beach. He heard Loretta's brother, Wayne, laughing with some other boys in the locker room after practice. They were talking about Henry.

"I buy them beer all the time," Wayne laughed. "Your sister has eyes for a chocolate boy, Pete, no doubt about it."

Pete confronted Birdie as he drove her to church. She assured him that she and Henry were only friends. They only drank one beer, just enough to relax and take them away from their worries. It wasn't like they sat on the beach and got drunk, not like his friends.

"What the hell do you have to worry about, Birdie? You're a princess in this family. They've been planning your debut since the day you were born. Snap out of it. You're going to shame our parents." Pete's jaw clenched, his knuckles turning white on the steering wheel. Birdie glanced at him then stared ahead. "Nobody thinks you're cool because you have a black friend. You're going to get him in big trouble. There are people around here who don't like that kind of thing, people who'd love an excuse to scare him and rough him up. If you don't break this off for your sake, do it for him."

Pete slammed the car door, leaving Birdie sitting inside in the sweltering heat. She knew he was right. There were people who would misconstrue their friendship, but she was determined not to let the prejudices of other people determine who her friends could be. She ran, following Pete into church where their parents waited in their familiar pew. Her mother stared at her, probably noticing her tense jaw and the sweat plastering her hair to her face. Birdie fidgeted with the hymnal, flipping the pages, her hands trembling with anger at Pete's words. Her mother placed her hand on Birdie's and shook her head when Birdie glanced at her. Birdie's hand stopped, but her insides roared.

The sermon was about loving thy neighbor. Birdie fumed, becoming angrier with each "amen." She glanced behind her to see Wayne sitting with his family. Loretta gave her a little wave. *This is bullshit.* Birdie got up and made her way to the back of the church, staring at the harvest gold carpet in front of her. She couldn't make eye contact with any of the other worshipers. Her parents probably thought she was going to the bathroom, but she stormed through the double doors and all the way home.

She threw her dress flats up on the porch as she thundered past the steps to the alley. She could feel the pebbles burying into her feet. Birdie stomped into the garage and pulled her bicycle down from the rack. She straddled it and began to pump as her stockings slipped against the pedals. Tears clouded her eyes as she dodged cars and headed toward the area north of Broadway.

Thirty minutes after leaving the church, Birdie was pushing her bicycle in front of Henry's apartment. Henry's mother opened the screen door and marched out to Birdie with a scowl. "Girl, you better think twice about what you're doing. I don't have to tell you how white folks feel about black boys. I'm sure you hear that ugly talk every day. You need to leave Henry alone."

Birdie looked past Henry's mom at a figure standing at the door.

She turned toward Birdie's gaze. "Go ahead. Go see what you've done to him. It's not right, and you know it." The woman's teeth shown in a sneer.

Birdie walked toward the apartment, noticing the cuts and swollen eyes the closer she got. She gasped when she was close enough to see Henry's bloodshot eyes. "What happened?" Birdie whispered. She held her hand to her throat and tears welled in her eyes.

"Some guys jumped me last night. T-bone and I were going floundering down backtrack, and these guys jumped us. They let him go. They were after me."

"Your eyes, what happened to your eyes?" Birdie sobbed.

"They don't hurt. It'll be okay. That's what happens when someone tries to choke you." Henry shrugged and scratched his forehead. "What are you doing over here anyway? You supposed to be in church?"

"I just had a feeling. Pete said something about Wayne, and I walked out of church and came here. I just had a bad feeling."

"Yeah, Wayne was one of them. They had bandanas tied across their faces, but I pulled his down. I thought it was him. I recognized his voice."

"You need to tell the police," Birdie cried. "You know who did this. Call the police."

Henry's mother hurried over to the door. "Get inside, Henry. Birdie, you need to go on home now. You don't understand. The police won't do anything. That boy's father is the district attorney. I'm not going to allow my boy to go through that. You get on home where you belong. It's about time you figured that out."

Birdie looked up at Henry, and he held his hands up behind his mother's back, indicating seven. She knew that was the sign to meet him at seven on the beach.

Birdie rode home, furious as she peddled recklessly down alleys, avoiding trash cans. She clenched her teeth and wiped the tears that obscured her vision. They would run away, she decided. She and Henry would hitchhike to Houston. She didn't know what they'd do, or where they'd stay, but Henry would help her figure it out.

Birdie threw her bicycle down in the front yard and stormed past Pete and up the stairs. He watched her from the front hall. Her mother brushed past him and called her name from the bottom of the stairs, but Birdie didn't answer. She stayed in her room during the fried chicken lunch her mother had prepared. She changed into jeans and a T-shirt. She'd wait until Sunday afternoon naps to slip out of the house again, somehow confident her family's routine would continue as normal despite her heartbreak. Birdie pushed clean underwear and a change of clothes into a backpack. She would be ready when Henry agreed to leave with her.

But it didn't happen. Henry had talked her out of running. "Mama's afraid of losing her job," he'd said. "She's worried this whole thing could cause more trouble. One of her coworkers has been let go for the same thing. People like us can't afford to get let go, Birdie."

"That's why we have to leave, Henry. Leave all these stupid people behind and start our own lives without them."

"There's stupid people everywhere, Birdie. It's not just here. Don't you watch the news? It doesn't matter that we're just friends. Wherever we go, people will think what they want and judge us. We have to make the best of what we have. At least people know us here."

"I don't want them to know me," Birdie cried. "And I don't want to know them."

"We have two more years of high school, Birdie. We can make it two more years."

"You could've been killed. Those boys could've killed you and they would've gotten away with it."

Henry laughed. "If they'd killed me, I imagine you'd be screaming from the top of Shearn Moody Plaza. They wouldn't get away with it. You're going to be a lawyer one of these days, Birdie. You'll find justice somewhere."

Not long after Birdie was back home, trying to sneak her bicycle back into the garage, her father appeared at the door with a suitcase in his hand. "Get in the car, Birdie. We're taking a trip."

She started to run, but Pete was standing behind her. He opened the back door of the car, blocking her way. She crawled in and began to cry herself to sleep. She had no idea where she was going.

When Birdie opened her eyes, she looked at the back of the heads of her parents and brother, shoulder to shoulder in the front seat of the sedan. This wasn't a family outing. They were taking her away. They were her enemies, the enemies of justice and anything that was fair.

Birdie stared at cold biscuits on her plate, feeling the lilting motion of the ship. Her coffee was cold and undrinkable, a black ring circling the inside of the white mug. She had the sinking feeling she would get when nothing seemed to be going right. Her thoughts could crowd the day with consequences, the penalties of everything she had ever done. Those moody thoughts had already ruined her breakfast. It didn't bode well for the rest of the day.

She didn't want to be near Loretta and be reminded of her brother. Birdie wouldn't listen to placating pleads to get happy in the same pants she got sad in, those tired words of her mother's. They were supposed to be her friends, but she wouldn't allow them to take Henry's memory and make something ugly out of it. She knew who he was, and she knew their special bond. She had paid the price for sticking up for Henry, and he'd paid a price also.

None of the threats and isolation made Birdie change her mind about Henry. To her, he was worth ten of his adversaries. It put a knot in her stomach to include her own family among those foes. Henry had fought for those people, given his life. Birdie was ashamed of her parents and her brother, embarrassed

that they never wanted to get to know the only person in her life
she could trust.

CHAPTER 40

JUDE

THE MARIJUANA WORKED. Jude was pleasantly surprised to find she was pain-free for substantial periods of time. She was able to be in the moment, sitting on the deck or on the beach enjoying the sun with Ollie and Barry. They enjoyed a couple of lazy days with no schedule or routine. They ate and slept when they wanted, paying no attention to light and dark

Barry and Jude walked the beach after sunset, listening to the waves and looking out at the moon sprinkling tiny lights on the surface of the sea. Barry built a fire in the fire pit, and they sat among the tall grasses in the dunes at the base of the house, sometimes dozing against the cushions from the deck furniture. They held skewers over the coals and roasted franks. Jude sat cross-legged and squirted mustard on the meat straight from the bottle, then licked her fingers.

She took long steamy showers for no reason and dried her hair on the deck in the swinging hammock before falling asleep with a book in her hand. Time was irrelevant, and she would swear she had no thoughts while she held her face to the breeze as Ollie would do. The clutter in her mind had been erased. There were no plans to be made, no preparations; everything was done. Jude looked at the palms of her hands and told herself, "That's all there is. There's no more to do.

"How did you know that's what I needed?" Jude said to Barry as he drove down the seawall to Birdie's. "You showed up at exactly the right time and had just what I needed."

Barry glanced to the back seat where Ollie was again holding his nose out the window to the breeze. He smiled. "I think it's because it's what I needed, too. It's been here all along: the brown bag in Birdie's freezer, the water, the moon, the sun, the nothingness of sitting above the dunes. It was always there."

"Yeah, it was." Jude yawned. She continued to feel the laziness of a still mind. Caring about what would happen next didn't occur to her.

Jude turned her face toward the water and rested her head on the headrest, her hair blowing out the window. Gentle tugs of breeze swirled the tendrils and flung them back against her face. She closed her eyes and allowed it. There was no reality, only the very essence of each thing around her: the breeze, the motion of the car, the music on the radio, the gulls laughing above them at stoplights. Jude separated each piece in her head, aware of every part.

Barry pulled his car into the alley and parked beside Birdie's in the garage. Ollie jumped from the back when Jude opened the door, heading into the courtyard to his outside water bowl. Jude threw her backpack over her shoulder and mounted the steps to the porch. Dark clouds grabbed her attention. They were in a thick heavy line, hanging in the northern sky. The air held an odor of sulfur. Jude tilted her head back and felt the change approaching.

"I'm glad we're back in town, off the beach," Barry said. "I think there's a storm coming. It's supposed to be cooler by morning."

"I'm ready for cool weather," Jude said. "Most of my clothing is for warm weather, but I guess I can make do." She grimaced. Uh, Barry do you have any more of those brownies. I'm feeling a little…."

"Sure, no problem. I left some here in the freezer."

Jude dropped her backpack on the porch and sat on one of the wicker chairs. Her stomach was knotting, and she was getting the panicked feeling of an approaching attack. She took a deep breath and let it out slowly, trying to breathe away the pain. She closed her eyes and sat with both hands on the arms of the chair.

"Here you go," Barry said. He held out a saucer with small squares of brownie and a glass of wine. Jude took the plate and set it on the table between them, then took the wine. She picked up a bit of brownie and ate it, slowly washing down the grit with wine. Barry joined her, taking small pieces. They watched as the cloud moved over them, and the wind picked up, blowing leaves from the trees in Birdie's courtyard.

The odor in the air changed from sulfur to rain, and then it began to pour. The rain blew within feet of where they were seated. Ollie got up and moved inside the house to his pillow. Jude and Barry remained on the porch, silently watching the storm. It began to lightning and thunder. As the rumbling of the storm grew louder, the tension in Jude's stomach eased and she became comfortable. She had no desire to move.

She wasn't sure how long they sat watching, not speaking, before Jude jumped at a loud knocking at the front door. She stood, looking toward Barry and shrugging. She walked to the dining room window and glanced out. There was a patrol car parked in front of the house.

Jude hurried back to the porch. "It's the cops, Barry," she whispered.

"Okay, wait until I put this plate in the fridge, and then answer the door."

Jude opened the door to Birdie's friend Eldon. "I'm sorry to disturb you, but I had some news I thought you'd like to hear," he said.

Barry motioned Eldon inside. He was dripping rain and stood on the mat inside the foyer. Jude's heart was racing. Her only thought was that something had happened to Birdie.

Eldon was dressed in his uniform. He took his hat off when he entered the house. "I wanted to let you know that we've confirmed the death of Jaxson Emile Tims. Travis County has notified our office that his motorcycle apparently left the road last night. They located his body this morning just outside of Bastrop. It's been confirmed from tattoos and identification on the body that it's Jaxson. I know you were worried that he might still be out there somewhere. I just thought you'd like to know."

Jude relaxed. She smiled at Eldon. "Thank you for taking the time to come and tell me. That is such a relief. I'm sorry he's dead, but I'm glad he's not stalking anyone to do them harm. I do appreciate this."

They chatted briefly about Birdie's trip, but Barry didn't encourage Eldon to linger. After closing the front door, Barry turned to Jude and let out a sigh. He started to grin, and Jude began to giggle. "We were almost busted, or is that paranoia?"

They both giggled. Jude's laugh became hysterical and tears rolled from her eyes. She clutched her side and eventually went to her knees in a full-blown cry. She sobbed in uncontrollable gasps. Barry stared at her in disbelief.

Jude tried to stop crying so she could assure Barry that she would be okay, but he was pacing, stopping only to put his hand on her shoulder to ask what was wrong. Finally he kneeled beside her and put his arm around her. Her head fell onto his chest, and she continued the gasping cries until they subsided into halting breaths and then silence. They continued to sit on the floor.

The first to move, Jude sniffed and apologized. She excused herself to get a tissue and Barry took his time getting up and returned to the kitchen to get his wine. He took the brownies from the refrigerator and stared out the back door at the pouring rain.

"That was a cleansing cry," Jude said. She walked up behind him, dabbing her eyes. "My heart raced every time I heard a motorcycle. I was so afraid he would find me. That was Casey's boyfriend, Jax. So now he's gone. One less thing to worry about."

"You okay?"

"Yes, I know that was weird. I don't know where it came from. I think it's a combination of this whole ...." Jude swirled her arms in the air, signifying she didn't know what. The whole adventure gone wrong—a mistake or fate, she didn't know which.

CHAPTER 41

BIRDIE

MAXINE CALLED BIRDIE'S name from the buffet. She waved and mouthed, "Come on," when Birdie looked up to find her. She was sluggish getting up. Her desire to participate in their plans for the day was waning. There were only two days left on the cruise, and the rest of the group wanted to make the most of it. Birdie, on the other hand, just wanted it to be over.

The coffee bar caught Birdie's eye, and she stopped and poured herself another cup of coffee. She had let her breakfast go cold and she was unfulfilled. There was something missing. She was hopeful hot coffee would be what she needed, but after one sip, she realized that wasn't it.

Maxine scowled at Birdie. "Now what are you going to do with a full cup of coffee. We have to go down to deck one to exit the ship. How are you going to manage that?" Maxine pointed to the cup in Birdie's hand and shook her head, frowning at Birdie.

"Maybe you should go on ahead without me. I'm not feeling too good," Birdie said. "If I decide to leave later, I'll catch up with you. I'd rather sit with a book in the solarium."

"Nonsense, Birdie. You paid good money for this excursion. Put that cup down and come on."

"No, no, I'm not coming. I told you I don't want to. Now go ahead, and don't argue with me. I'll be fine. I just want to rest a while."

"Was it what Loretta said last night? You've been acting funny ever since."

"Go, Maxine. You'll be late. Just go."

Maxine shook her head and sighed, leaving Birdie standing next to a waiter with a tray of mimosas. Birdie waited until Maxine was out of sight and took one of the drinks from the tray. Later, as Birdie sat with her book in the solarium, she saw her friends walking up the dock toward town. *It looks hot as hell out there.* She was glad she chose to remain on board.

The thought that Maxine was complaining to Betty and Loretta crossed Birdie's mind, but she didn't care. They could gossip about her if they wanted. She was used to being the subject of gossip. Would they decide she was crazy because she was a lesbian, or would they decide her friendship with Henry drove her crazy? It certainly couldn't be the injustice in the world that pissed her off.

Birdie closed her eyes. She finally felt relaxed, not trying to pretend.

The moodiness was a constant in her life. It had been with her for as long as she could remember. As long as the people around her were neutral about her friends and associations and accepted her creativity as part of her, she was fine, but the minute anyone questioned her friendship with Henry, sexualized it in any way, or questioned Jude's motives in wanting to be her friend, she bristled. She tended to focus on the unkind words, ruminating on them until they felt like poison in her mouth. Stirring the pain, judgment, and sour memories in with her resentment, she created her own funk. She could accept some responsibility for part of her sentiment; however, she needed someone besides herself to blame.

The responsibility, Birdie thought, should fall on those people who refused to get to know another person, a person worthy of knowing, like Henry. Those people—her parents, her brother, and her friends—should suffer for not knowing her Henry. It wasn't enough that they didn't get to know him—their loss, Birdie thought. She wanted them to suffer for it. After all the years since Henry's death, Birdie couldn't get over the fact that he was no longer there for her, and those who claimed to

302

love her would never know him; she mourned that, and she mourned Henry. But when she shut her eyes, she still had that spirit. He was still there.

The notion that Henry could be with her in a more acceptable form to those around her bothered Birdie. It made her even angrier than never having that spirit again. She would have to share it because now, everyone would want to be with such a spirit. They would flock to it, and she would be left in the background, trying to gain attention. *There is no pleasing me.* Birdie's frustration was just as intense about herself as it was for the friends who didn't understand her. *It's not easy to be with me.*

Birdie nodded off in a deck chair on the shaded side of the ship. It was quiet and she had drained the mimosa. She was vaguely aware of the people at the other end of the row of chairs, but she allowed herself to dream and withdraw from the others in the solarium.

Birdie walked her bicycle along the neglected tracks, abandoned behind the warehouses. Henry was supposed to meet her there. She had sardines and crackers in her backpack. It was still light, but she had a flashlight. She looked across the stagnant pool of water not far from motionless train cars. The sun was setting and reflecting on the still pool, the odor of the sea life swelling in the air under the viaduct.

Later in the warehouse, Birdie and Henry sat in a damp corner on crates. He brought two bottles of beer. Henry always opened them with his teeth, smiling after handing Birdie one of the bottles. "Why is it I always have to listen to you tell me about the injustice in the world and I'm the one who should be complaining to you?" Henry asked.

"Cause you never complain about anything," Birdie pouted. "You never think there's anything wrong."

"That's not true. I know there's more wrong than there is right, but I want to focus on what's right. Jeez, Birdie, if I worried as much about all that shit as you do, I'd be crazy. Sometimes you just have to go with the flow, you know?"

"Never," Birdie insisted. "I'll never think it's okay to be such an asshole."

"The world has a mixture of people. You can judge and be judged. That's what it's all about. Can't we just eat sardines and enjoy being in a big warehouse without people telling us what to do for a few minutes? Do we have to wallow in it even while we're hiding from it?"

"That's probably why we're friends, Henry. We're different."

"Yeah, but we're the same. The same because we're different."

Birdie was roused by someone dragging a chair across the floor. She swallowed the dryness in her throat and knew that's when she was supposed to stop dreaming. Henry had said what she was meant to hear.

She glanced around her. A group had gathered close by. Picking up her book, she walked past the people laughing in the hot tub. She found the self-serve coffee and water and filled a glass with ice and water. A bleached-blonde with round, black glasses tried to make small talk, but Birdie smiled and nodded before walking away as if she didn't understand what she was talking about. That was the beauty of a cruise —she could pretend she didn't speak English.

People were milling around, gathering to prepare for the noon meal. Birdie found a table in the back with only two chairs, less likely to attract anyone needing to share a space. She put her book down and remained standing to glance at the dock. She spotted them coming toward the ship, Maxine, Loretta, and Betty. Betty was carrying bags—T-shirts, Birdie supposed. She sat down, not wanting them to spot her standing near the glass.

Birdie thought she would have a few minutes of respite before they deposited their purchases and started searching for her. *Wonder why they didn't eat in town?*

A few more minutes of time by myself. She closed her eyes after taking a sip of cold water.

When she returned, Jude would want to leave and find a place of her own. She didn't want her to leave, certain that Jude's spirit and Henry's were one and the same. *There is a reason he has come back to me, but he may not know what it is.*

She thought they had come full circle twice. There was something she was supposed to do. She had wasted her life being pissed that she was different, avoiding involvement, finding reasons not to engage. Surely that wasn't all there was to her life. There was something else.

CHAPTER 42

JUDE

TWO DAYS BACK in Birdie's house and Jude knew she had lost a significant amount of weight. Her favorite jeans barely hung on her hips. She looked at her face in the mirror; her cheeks were sunken, and her eyes appeared flat. She forced herself to smile in the mirror, but there was still a vacancy behind her gaze. She barely recognized herself.

Food was no longer appealing. Jude had to coerce herself to eat, unable to enjoy meals. There was no strength or desire to tackle the painting project she'd planned to complete before Birdie's return.

The pain in Jude's stomach began to increase, and she bent at the waist, unable to stand erect. She slumped to the floor and sat there with her head on the side of the tub. The cold porcelain felt comfortable on her cheek. Jude remained seated, her eyes closed. She wondered if she had the strength to stand and make her way downstairs. She could hear Barry and smell the coffee wafting to the second floor. The aroma that once motivated her to go downstairs repelled her. She heard Ollie's tags jingling on his collar. He was coming up. His nails clicked against the wood floors in the hall, and then she saw him standing in the doorway, looking at her.

Ollie rarely ventured upstairs. He watched her from the hall and then hung his head and walked slowly toward her. Jude couldn't lift her head from the tub. Her eyes felt heavy, but she smiled at Ollie. He sought her out, and she knew he was aware that she would be leaving soon. Jude watched as Ollie curled up next to her feet and closed his eyes. She ran her fingers across the wispy fur on the scruff of his neck. He moaned and stretched closer to her, twisting his head to face her. Rolling his eyes, he gave her a mournful look—his eyes pleading something she could only guess.

Unaware how long they'd been in silence, Jude heard someone coming up the stairs. Soon, Barry appeared at the door. He held a plate of small cubes of brownies. Closing the toilet lid, Barry sat down and held the plate in front of Jude. She took a small piece and nibbled on it without speaking. She knew Barry didn't need her to say anything; they had learned to understand each other without speaking. It was ironic that she found someone, a soul mate, just as she was leaving the world.

Ollie opened his eyes and watched, then stood and shook, heading out the bathroom door and down the hall. Jude could hear his tags jingling again as he bounced down the stairs.

Barry sat with her, a glass of ice water in his hand. When she glanced at him, he held the water up and raised his eyebrows. Jude supposed he didn't have the energy to speak either. Since the previous evening, they had said little, and Jude knew he understood her aversion to words. There was nothing to explain the end of a life; it just hung between them, unexplainable. They could move each other to tears with words, and she was tired of tears dried on her pillow. They soaked her thoughts with regrets, victories, and mysteries. She wondered if she would see her mother, Casey, her father, anyone she knew when she finally let go.

Jude closed her eyes, allowing the cannabis to filter through her body. She wanted to hang on until Birdie returned. She wanted to tell her something. There was a scene behind her eyes, a peaceful beach with a bicycle. Two silhouettes were seated near the water. The waves lapped at them, coming just close enough to threaten but never touching. She knew she was one of the silhouettes. She was there in that shadow of a body, the essence of the being. She wasn't the darkness of the thing but the brightness around it, the aura. She watched as their heads tilted in conversation, but she couldn't hear the voices.

As they spoke, the light became brighter around the other body. Jude knew who it was. Then she knew it didn't matter who it was. It was a soul becoming enlightened, and that was why she was there.

Barry shifted and Jude raised her head. "I'm going to shower and put on clothes," she insisted.

"Are you sure? You should be comfortable, Jude. Don't worry about clothes."

"I'm sure. Birdie's coming today, right? I have something to tell her. I want to make sure she thinks I'm coherent."

Barry laughed, then held his hand out to help Jude stand. "I'll be on the stairs. Leave the door open in case you need help." He left the room.

What would I have done if Barry hadn't stopped by after Birdie left? It was fate, she thought, that he returned. He must've had an intuition. She wondered, while she was under the running water, how the universe conspired to make things happen.

She twisted her hair into a knot and secured it with a clip before she applied lip gloss. She rubbed her finger across the palette and smoothed some on her cheeks, a suggestion of what could be there.

Barry was seated on the stairs, his back to her as she crossed the hall to slip into a sundress and sweater. She started down the stairs barefoot as Barry stood. Jude followed him into the den, where he placed the water on a table beside an easy chair. He picked up her sandals and held them on the tips of his fingers. "I can rub your feet with that lotion you like and buckle your shoes."

"That would be great." Jude sat down in the chair and put her feet on the ottoman. "Are you okay with picking Birdie up later?"

"Of course." Barry squeezed a dollop of lotion onto his palm and began massaging Jude's calves and feet. "Birdie will be okay, Jude. She's a tough cookie, always has been."

"I know she will. I really wanted to do that painting for her, just a token of my appreciation for all her help. I'm not worried about Birdie. I've known her twice in her lifetime, and I know I'll see her again and again. I'm looking forward to it."

"Twice? I didn't know you had known Birdie before. I thought you just met on the beach a few weeks ago?"

"It's a long story. Birdie knows it. She said something to me before she left. The silly things she worried about during this life have nothing to do with her future. She'll figure it out."

"I'm not so sure you're speaking as coherently as you wanted there, Jude," Barry chuckled.

"Don't make fun of a person with one foot on the other side, Barry. You ever wonder these past few days why we didn't meet before now?"

"Yeah, I have. But I was just thinking while you were talking that we'll probably see each other again, too."

"We will. We certainly will. I'll make sure of it.

CHAPTER 43

BIRDIE & JUDE

BIRDIE SAW HER car and squinted at the driver, wondering why Barry had arrived to pick her up at the dock. Her heart raced, questions forming behind her worried eyes. She greeted him as the trunk opened. He hugged her briefly and heaved her bag inside.

"These are the treats I bought." Birdie handed him a shopping bag tied together with ribbon at the handles. "Where's Jude?" Birdie asked, tilting her head up and looking through the bottom of the lenses of her new sunglasses.

"She's waiting at the house. She's anxious for you to be home, and so is Ollie."

"It's good to be home. I'm ready for my own bed and home-cooked food. We don't have to wait for Maxine. She caught a ride with Loretta."

Barry drove in silence out of the parking lot at the dock. When he turned onto Harborside, he said, "Uh, Aunt Birdie, Jude hasn't been feeling well."

"I knew that was coming. I was afraid of it. I just thought she might have months instead of weeks. I shouldn't have gone on the cruise."

"No, I believe she would tell you that you did exactly the right thing. She's having a good day today, and she's up and waiting for you to get home. I've been with her. I had taken some time off anyway. It all worked out."

Birdie turned in the seat and looked at Barry. "What do you mean, you've been with her? You've been staying at the house with her?"

"Not like that, Aunt Birdie. Your mind always goes to the most offensive place." Barry hit the blinker a little harder than he intended, frustrated that he had to answer to Birdie. "I had rented a beach house with some buddies and I was here anyway."

"You didn't tell me you were going to do that."

"I don't have to tell you every little thing. Oh, and by the way, we've been eating your brownies and smoking your pot." Barry glanced in the rearview mirror with a sly grin on his face. "Eldon came by one day while we were …."

"Sweet baby Jesus, Barry! I leave for a week and you've broken into—"

"Calm down. It's okay. It really helped the pain for Jude. It was just the thing she needed, and it's kept her from being debilitated."

"I didn't even know you knew about that. For heaven's sake, what else do you know?"

"It doesn't matter. All that matters is Jude is free of pain and you're home. We don't need to fight today about your stash, Birdie."

"Pull over!"

"No, I won't. Calm down, Birdie."

"Pull over, right there at The Blooms. I'm going to get some flowers. I am calm, Barry. Pull over. Flowers in the house will be nice."

Barry eased over and parked in front of a flower shop. Birdie exited the car, slamming the door. Barry rubbed his forehead, his elbow resting on the ledge of the window. He had forgotten how trying it was for him to carry on a conversation with Birdie. He hoped she would be different with Jude; he didn't want their reunion to be stressful.

Barry watched as Birdie followed a woman out of the shop with an armful of pale pink flowers wrapped in tissue paper.

Birdie was talking to the woman, but he couldn't hear what she was saying.

Birdie opened the back door and put the flowers down on the seat, then got into the front seat, smiling. "I wish peonies grew down here. They are the most beautiful flower, but it's too hot here for them." Barry felt like he had missed something. Birdie's mood was no longer confrontational.

"What do you think Jude will feel like eating for lunch?" Birdie asked.

"I don't know. Her appetite's suffered, but she's liked that soup you put up for her."

"I'll make another pot. Stop at George's and I'll go in and get a few things."

Barry followed Birdie's directions all the way home and unpacked the car per her instructions as she mounted the steps to the back porch to greet Ollie.

Birdie's eyes teared as she spotted Jude in the easy chair, her head back and her eyes closed. She tiptoed past her and put the flowers in a vase, placing it beside Jude's chair. Birdie waited beside the chair, watching Jude's chest move with each breath. She was much thinner than the day she'd dropped Birdie and Maxine off at the dock. Her hands were bony and frail, clutched around the front of her sweater.

Birdie leaned closer. There was a red string tied around one of Jude's wrists.

Jude stirred, blinking slowly. "Birdie? You're home. Do I look a sight? You look like you've seen a ghost."

"That's my favorite dress, Jude. I am returned from the ocean. I was looking at that string tied around your wrist, and thinking about a friend of mine who used to do such a thing."

"It was Henry, wasn't it?" Jude said.

"Yes, it was. How did you know that?" Birdie gave a slight smile, her eyes squinted a little, a twinkle of curiosity in them.

"You know very well how I know, Birdie. I heard you say things about Henry before you left. You know me."

"I know you both." Birdie pointed to the flowers sitting beside the chair. "Aren't these lovely? I thought they would be a nice homecoming touch."

Birdie pulled a wilted leaf from one of the stems. She cleared her throat. "Henry's mother's family was from some islands near Jamaica. She had customs she still practiced from there. When she was concerned about her children, afraid they might be in danger, she tied a red string around their wrists. Henry often wore such a wristlet. Now here you sit with the same amulet."

Jude lifted her hand and stared at the string. Her eyes were glassy, the lids heavy from sleep. "I don't know why I tied this to my wrist, but I thought it would help me stay alert for your return. Birdie, I can go to the emergency room and get checked into the hospital. I know I'm shutting down. I can die there, not in this house."

"Nonsense," Birdie cried. "That's hogwash, Jude. I won't hear of it. You will be right here with me. I won't be inconvenienced with having to sit by your side in the hospital away from Ollie and my house. I'm making soup, and you'll be in my bed downstairs. You have no business trailing up those steps to bed. I would welcome your ghost in this house, but this is not the day for it. Your spirit will soar. The doors are open and will stay that way. Shush that talk of hospials."

Jude gave a faint smile, lacking the energy to curl her lips into a full grin. She didn't need to argue. Birdie recognized the effort and patted her shoulder as she went into the kitchen.

Jude closed her eyes and ran her fingers through Ollie's fur. He had jumped onto the chair and curled up beside her.

Birdie wiped the tears from her eyes as she stood at the sink. She looked up and shook her head as Barry brought the groceries into the kitchen. He nodded and put the bags on the counter, and then headed out the French doors to retrieve Birdie's luggage.

Birdie braced herself with both hands as she leaned against the counter. She stood with her eyes closed, feeling an energy surround her. Her hands tingled and a wave of sensation traveled up her arms, over her shoulders, to the top of her head.

"What are you doing, Birdie?" Jude said in a loud whisper from the next room.

"I'm going to make some soup." Birdie wiped her nose and walked back into the den. She smiled when she saw Ollie cuddled next to Jude. "He always has liked you."

"He has an intuition about me, like all animals do. I just realized we've been together before. It was in another life, a full life. We were free, unencumbered, running here and there. I saw us in a dream. He looked different and so did I, but it was us. I saw you and me, too, Birdie. We were sitting on the beach, talking."

"Yes, we always did that." Birdie nodded.

"We sat on the beach so the waves could pound around the sounds of our voices. Sometimes we would shout our anger and frustration to the sea, watch it slither in the white foam back out into the depths of the ocean. Sometimes we would sit there for hours, saying nothing, letting the sea shout at us. The surf would scream to us. Remember it would say 'Everything will be okay in the end, and if it's not okay, it's not the end.'" Birdie said in a soft voice.

"I do remember," Jude struggled to whisper. "Guess what, Birdie? This is a bit of an end. I'm supposed to tell you there is such a thing as life everlasting, but it's not what you think. You don't float around with angels in clouds, weightless, and vacant. You're an angel, always and forever. In your lime-green crop pants and that silly straw hat you wear. You're an angel in that deep debutant bow you practiced in secret in your robe. You're an angel bending over me on the beach. You're an angel laughing with Maxine about Loretta's bright lipstick. You've always been an angel in this life, and the ones before, and the next. Your parents, your friends, your appearance, your sexuality, your skin color, they will always be different, but you will always be an angel. Because, Birdie, you aren't those things. You're a soul, and the soul is what each living being is. Some people call it God."

Jude sighed as Birdie stared at her. She had exhausted her body delivering the speech. She closed her eyes. "I came back here just for this moment, to tell you don't fret the lives you will have. Live them, and don't fret the lives that have gone before. They are your lessons, your chores."

Birdie sat on the ottoman, looking at Jude. "I have a question." Jude's eyes remained shut, but fluttered beneath the lids. "Did you get to choose this life, the one you have now?"

"I think I volunteered," Jude agreed. "My soul longed. It longed to be here with you, and now... it's time.

Birdie gasped and clutched Jude's hand. She held it and twirled the red string between her fingers. Tears fell onto her arm. She watched as Jude's chest continued to rise and fall in breath, then slowed.

Ollie put his chin on Jude's leg, resting it there and looking to Birdie. He sighed and closed his eyes. There was a low gurgle, and then Jude's chest was still.

Barry stood behind the chair, watching Birdie.

"She's gone, Barry," Birdie said, wiping her eyes.

"Yes, I know. I'm sorry Birdie. I'll call Eldon. He can tell us who to contact."

Ollie jumped down from the chair when Birdie stood. He went out the back door onto the porch.

Birdie paced, tears in her eyes. *Again, again they're leaving me. Again, I'm left. Barry and I, we're the only ones who continue. But that's not true. Jude said, Henry said, we go on. We are connected and we move between these lives, as angels.*

The phone rang. Birdie squeezed her eyes shut. She had no use for anyone on the other end of that ringing. It made no sense. She followed the noise to the phone on the kitchen counter, staring at the number and the name—Maxine. *I won't answer that. I don't know what to say. I'll ignore it. It is something I can ignore.*

She went back to Jude, placing her hand on Jude's forehead. It was cool to the touch.

The sounds in the house were foreign, making no sense. Birdie walked to the door of her room. Barry had placed her luggage just inside the door. She wanted Jude to have the room. She'd planned to move to the guest room on the second floor. She'd wanted Jude to be there, sleeping, waking to make the coffee. Birdie would smell the aroma and put her robe on. None of the things she wanted would happen. She paced, the things that wouldn't happen making her angry.

Walking to the French doors, Birdie saw Ollie standing on the edge of the porch, his nose held in the air, sniffing. She walked to stand beside him, tilting her head up, her chin jutted toward the sound of surf. Tears flowed down her cheeks. She bent her head and said the only prayer she knew, then turned and sat in one of the chairs.

There was a commotion from inside the house, Barry's voice and someone else. It was Eldon with the coroner. Birdie walked inside and stood beside Jude, touching her one more time, caressing her hair, then turning to allow the coroner and those behind him access to her. Barry followed her onto the porch.

"She had a peaceful time while you were gone, Aunt Birdie." Barry told her about the beach house and their lazy days there. He said she'd intended to paint the dining and living rooms. He assured her that Jude's pain was managed, and she was satisfied that she had a purpose and was supposed to be on the beach when Birdie found her.

Birdie nodded. "It doesn't make it less sad, though, does it? It doesn't make me less mad either. Why do I always have to be the one left behind? Promise me, Barry, promise me you will let me leave you."

CHAPTER 44

BIRDIE & JUDE

FIVE YEARS AFTER Jude's death, Barry sat in the dining room going through boxes of photos. There were Polaroids, yellowed with age. He weeded out the ones with no people, tossing them into the garbage can next to the table. He suspected they were taken by Birdie. He could see a resemblance to Maxine and Betty in the faces of the young girls in the photos. They wore bell-bottom jeans, wide bands holding their long straight hair back from their foreheads, and their lips were painted with pale pink lipstick.

Barry grinned at the photos of his mother and father, clowning for Birdie's camera. The beach scenes were nostalgic: Birdie's bicycle parked in the sand, a tall black boy with a modest afro standing beside it. He was sitting on the rock groin, standing next to a Mardi Gras float in the krewe warehouse, and fishing under the viaduct, waving and smiling for the camera. In each of the photos there was a circle of light, a small orb, always on his right shoulder.

Barry flipped back through the photos. There was no mistake—it was the same consistent light. He dug other photos from the trash, examining the area for the same orb. It wasn't there.

Barry shook his head, continuing to examine the contents of the box. He found newer photos, some of Birdie's cruise. They had probably been printed from her phone. He smiled as he looked at Birdie and her friends dressed for dinner, smiling with martinis in their hands. They stood on the deck posing at the beginning of the trip.

Barry's hands began to shake as he picked up a photo of Birdie and Jude standing next to the car, Birdie's luggage on the sidewalk next to the open trunk. There was a circle of light on Jude's right shoulder. He ran his finger over the spot. Jude was smiling, looking healthier than he had known her.

Barry moved the box to his lap and it teetered there as he continued to pour through the photos. There were more of Birdie's trip. Then there was one of Jude seated in a chair, getting a pedicure in a salon. She held a glass of wine up to the camera. It was there, the orb, in the same spot.

Barry took his glasses off and rubbed his eyes. Birdie was gone. He had kept his promise. She got to leave him. A year later, he still missed her. Ollie was gone, too. There was nothing in the old house that he wanted to keep, and the realtor was coming to prepare a contract for sale. For some reason, he thought he should look at the box in the top of Birdie's closet.

Something had happened. Barry didn't think it was magic, because that would be hard to explain, but something more captivating and powerful had happened. Birdie hinted at it, Jude alluded to it, but he thought Birdie was daft and Jude was sick. Whatever mystery they had together, whatever charm or attraction, they took it with them—he couldn't explain it. Until he saw the photos, he had some doubts about the connection between Birdie and Jude. Their final conversation had been cryptic and whispered in tones he couldn't hear.

Barry took the photos he wanted to keep and put them in a small box next to his overnight bag. He took the popsicle box, putting it in the side pocket of his bag.

Glancing around the kitchen, Barry pictured Birdie puttering and mumbling, preparing a meal and grumbling about his insistence on accompanying her to church. He smiled to himself, remembering her. Wherever she was, he hoped she was with Henry or Jude and Ollie. He was sure whoever she was with would be listening to her, consoling her as she raged at an injustice, and admiring her. He knew he would be with her again someday.

He put a box and his bag on the dining room table. He wanted to do one more inspection of the upstairs before the realtor arrived. Barry stepped into the upstairs guest room, the one Jude had occupied. The bed had been stripped but all of the furniture was still there. There were only three drawers in a chest beside the bed. Something pulled him to the chest to inspect the drawers.

In the bottom drawer, Barry found a plastic grocery bag full of money and a note. Apparently Birdie had never looked in the drawer. He knew instantly what he would do with the money after talking with Eldon about it. There would be a scholarship awarded in the names of Birdie and Henry from a foundation funded by Jude. Barry would make it happen.

Other Books by Phyllis H. Moore

Sabine, Book One of a Series

Billy's Story, Book Two of a Series

Josephine's Journals, Book Three of a Series

Secrets of Dunn House, Book Four of a Series

Tangled, a Southern Gothic Yarn

Opal's Story

The Bright Shawl, Colors of Tender Whispers

And the Day Came

The Ember Months

Retirement, Now What? (nonfiction)

Follow me on:

My website: http://www.phyllishmoore.com

Amazon: https://www.Amazon.com/author/phyllishmoore

Pinterest

Facebook

GoodReads

BookBub

Thank you for reading *Birdie & Jude.* If you enjoyed this story, you might like *Opal's Story.* The reviews have been positive. Here are a few:

Great story......so believable!

The innocence we had back then....the prejudices ...the small town ...Good read! Will definitely recommend to my reading friends. Look forward to reading more from this author.

This book is a real page-turner. It has lots of twists and turns, leaving you wondering what will happen next. The characters are well developed and the plot moves along quickly, alternating between the past and the present. If you're from Texas (or anywhere in the South), you'll recognize and enjoy most of the local expressions used in the dialogue and you'll probably know some "real" people like the ones described in this book.

This is my favorite Phyllis H. Moore book so far! I felt like I was at the table with this family, I didn't want to put it down. I had to know how Opal's Story was going to unfold. Love the characters.

I made a mistake when I picked up Opal's Story - it was 3 days before Thanksgiving and I had plenty to do...Opal got more attention than the turkey. This is a story with a lot of foreshadowing, or so I thought. From the very beginning I thought I had it figured out, but there are twists and turns and additions to this little gem that were unexpected. The 3 main family-member characters are well developed and easily identifiable as the people they are - folksy and good-hearted. Opal has an extra dimension, but then it's all about her. I finished it yesterday on a car trip - missed Opal the minute I finished the book. This is my second Phyllis H. Moore book to read. I look forward to more from this fresh voice.